History of Fun

Published by
Mandrake of Oxford
PO Box 250
OXFORD
OX1 1AP (UK)

A CIP catalogue record for this book is available from the British Library and the US Library of Congress.

ISBN 1 869928636

Printed & bound by Antony Rowe Ltd, Eastbourne

History of Fun

Book I

by

Mary Hedger

Mandrake of Oxford
Specialist Independent Publishers
Since 1986

To you - unknown, unseen -

I believe in you

Contents

Chapter 8

Chapter 9

Chapter 10

Chapter 11

Chapter 12

Chapter 13

Chapter 14

Chapter 15

Chapter 1

1.1 Est, The Past

The room was spacious and red; large uncurtained windows led out to a junk littered balcony. Est and her lover stood by the TV. He rolled a torn rectangle of silver foil around a pencil to make a pipe. The tips of his fingers trembled slightly and her eyes glowed with excitement as he laid out two lines of brown heroin upon a second piece of foil. This was their communicant, to carry messages soul to soul.

She wore a high waisted doll style dress. Her long hair was held back from moon white face by an Alice band. She wore no make up. As he held a cigarette lighter under the foil, the powdered heroin melted and ran down the aluminium in a shiny brown smear. The smell of poppy was sweet and intoxicating. Est sucked wisps of grey smoke hard into her lungs and held it there. Tension dissolved into light and warmth, harbingers of the transformative power of heroin's charisma.

The strong drug invaded her mind, initiating whispered strands of words; 'The end is nigh, the end is rich. A hungry search towards the year 2000 and beyond, marking the end of all clothes other than Lycra and the end of all mothers other than Lillian: Lillian, who kisses like a virgin fantasising a future of 5,000 lovers: Lillian, Scarlet Woman, Rider of the Storm.'

In the shadowy bedroom Est moved slowly in response to her lover. She made strange high-pitched noises inaudible to the human ear, formulated to arouse deep inner muscles. His outstretched hand touched her body and lingered as if within an eddy sheltered from an emphatic tide.

Her lover came closer, to kiss her. His sulphurous breath was upon her. His tongue lingered along her gums and licked her lips.

He moaned softly, 'Oh your lips, your lips.'

As torpor overwhelmed her, the last thing she remembered apart from the appalling cliché she was living through, was the hideous sight of him scratching at himself.

1.2   Est, The Present

Est stood before her canvas in the candlelit room where she worked. Feet passed by on the street outside. She boldly wielded her brush and made bright, confident strokes. She was altogether elsewhere, painting herself and her daughter Claudia, to another, richer, dimension. Not struggling, something deeper than that, she engaged total imaginative control over her future. Her painting itself was a magickal act of Will, and in this she was like her Magician. She painted him as an impressive male figure; his intellectuality implied in the movements of colour upon canvas. She imagined the man within her picture as real and told him her previous night's dream:

'This dream is about how fate works when you have your back to the wall and how that wall hurts.

'When I first saw it I believed it to be the west wall in a house where five gangsters lived. But as I thought about it, it was replaced by a five metre high mesh fence, the gauge so fine that a finger could not pass through. I crashed into the fence and expected to be lying at its foot in pain, but I was not; I was knocking at a grey door marked 10X. It was the smartest door in a long row of battered front doors on the 7th floor of a 16 floor apartment block on the sea front. Everybody had gone to live at the seaside so building had taken place on an immense scale.

'I knock upon this front door, suspecting it's the door where

The Magician is spending his last days. I believe myself to be his heir. I am applying for the position. For I am "the soul that startles innocent eyes of blue/as they watch my wantonness seeping through," and so on. Vehicle of a holy mystery. Aloof and alone, unknown fire within brooding. Brooding on you mainly, Magician.'

Est stepped back from her canvas and squinted at her creation as the candle spluttered out. She laughed easily, pleased with her work. She placed her paintbrushes in turpentine and wiped her hands on a once white apron. She shook her hands vigorously to relieve hardworking fingers and looked about for grooming tools to make herself presentable to pick Claudia up from school.

She pulled her coat around her and buttoned it. Outside she screwed her eyes up at the bright sunlight after the cosy gloom of her basement apartment. As she locked the door behind her, her mood conjured a few ancient Babylonian stanzas:

> Dead men covered the approaches,
> The walls were gaping,
> The high gates, the roads
> Were piled with dead.

> In the side streets,
> Where feasting crowds would gather,
> Scattered they lay.

> In all the streets and roadways
> Bodies lay.
> In open fields that used to fill with dancers,
> They lay in heaps.
> The country's blood now filled its holes,
> Like metal in a mould,
> Bodies dissolved - like fat left out in the sun.

1.3   The Magician

The Magician mixed with many but remained aloof. Not an aloofness of snobbery or independence but of a real and cultivated difference.

He'd followed the alchemists' trail and become invincible; down the route of the writer he'd found the arrogance to sustain self-belief. Thus he had created a seemingly divine barrier between himself and the rest of humanity.

He needed to be consumed by love. During his early magickal experiments fine wines and cognac had been sufficient to maintain euphoria; liberally administered to his female assistant, his Scarlet Woman, naturally. He had moved on, medicinally, to heroin and cocaine. What in these modern days we have come to know as the *speedball,* as in, "I've done a speedball and I'm ready to die." His hourly companion was a pipeful of hashish but it's better not to talk about that for there is nothing to say about it.

Sometimes his mind was troubled, at such times he reached out for prophecy. What confused his mind? How could he further develop his already formidable Will to exactly command the future?

With night came chaos, one of the five superlative passions. Chaos! She who rides, proud head thrown back, inner thighs gripping horseflesh. Lillian, Scarlet Woman, she of magnificent abandon, of lasciviousness, would give her body to whosoever lusted uniquely.

He snuggled into her arms, crawled between her legs. She had poison tucked inside her gaiter; she dipped a tiny silver spoon into the phial and offered white powder to his quivering nostrils. He snorted the cocaine; it cleared his head and sexual prowess was his.

He fondled her pink shoulders, smelt her armpit which bore the dead flat odour of one who breathed thin expensive air, whose life ebbed and flowed at such rapid pace that there was no time for rarefication of any soul element.

He liked the smell of her. It didn't remind him of anything at all. There was nothing whatsoever maternal about her; she was a dead end, a cul-de-sac. She was her body. She had no soul. He liked it like that.

He liked to feed her alcohol, to numb her, and then direct her mind to the astral. She lost her soul at his persuasion, an alchemical achievement preceding another successful experiment. She went willingly to the laboratory defined by his Will, for the rituals gave her life meaning.

1.4 Est, Archetype or Stereotype?

Est paced her studio, paint brush in hand. 'I dream of enjoying country and city pleasures, in obedience to spiritual demands. Then comes the rapture, rarest sense of all, rapture of 17 hours in your arms. Yet you doubt the sincerity of my emotions. How so? When I, wanton creature that I am, have not shared passion for six infinite years?

'Magician, you are a strong and devilish presence, a dark cloak enwrapping my desires, those disparate threads of my jungle life. I have been chaste for six infinite years to purify myself for this righteous hunt.

'Infinite as galaxies, yes! When will you come to me at your most powerful and unreal? I am ready for you, ripe for you, because I no longer rely on my five sensory organs to define my feelings or sculpt my life.

'Magician, how I long for you! Can you sense the intensity of my desire?'

In this manner Est called Drummond, exuberant Priest of Pan, named The Beast, devil incarnate, dedicated to the appalling habit of guzzling elemental power. Est, dislocated from her physicality, searched for meaning within the curious dreams with which she had been riddled since infancy. She was intensely aware of him, while he was aware more of appetite.

Whose priestess was Est? This question tormented her as a plethora of possibilities confused her in a whirling throng of divinities; many had made an appearance during her spiritual development.

In spite of her preoccupation with the otherworldly, her nails grew as other nails did, her hair had to be arranged, an outfit assembled. There was work to be done, a bed to be slept in, aired and tidied.

What type of person was Est? She avoided fish while intuiting the necessity of seafood for peak health. Sat upon a grassy slope, fantasising that she ran in a poppy filled meadow. She fed birds while dreaming of butterflies. Ambiguity was natural to her, she curled up in an old armchair, knowing she'd be more comfortable near the fire upon a footstool.

She imagined a cottage and its garden at midnight. Scenes merged: where she was and where she imagined herself to be became as one and it came to her, the feeling of wolves. 'True fear is the fear that one's true inner self will manifest. Free will,' her reverie continued. 'How bleak a concept without fleshy correspondence! How dismal human nature when you can put a collar round its neck and watch it enjoy its enslavement after token rebellion!'

'Am I a drug?' she continued to ponder while disinterestedly putting on her coat (she was going out to buy wine). 'And as a drug will my influence upon him decline with familiarity?' She assumed that The Magician felt her within his personality and daily chores as minutely as she him, an assumption without foundation, in fact. Nothing unusual about that, most of Est's life was propelled by imagination. There were a few functions she performed with her fingers that were pretty much grounded in the here and now, like picking up a paintbrush or a cup.

She shut the door behind her and slipped out into the street, damp with soft rain. English greys in a thousand shades adorned sky and pavement.

A quick spasm of pain ran through her head as her pupils constricted in response to bright outside light after the gloom of her narrow hallway. Her mind was with The Magician. 'We will spend 17 hours in bed. It doesn't come up very often. Is 17 our lucky number? Is there a lottery ticket we're fighting over? Do we both know where a million pound lottery ticket sits unclaimed on a pensioner's mantel?

'And when we kiss, emotions will form within my lips. It'll be sad when we say goodbye; you'll become diminutive. I'll panic that I'm never going to see you again. Then your reassurances will make me feel I'm floating in mist. I won't recognise myself, I'll be so relaxed.'

'I still don't know who nor where you are. Gradually you will show me your secrets. I will enjoy taking your clothes off in daylight on the creaky bed and stroking your warm tummy. Later on, my fingers will make you musical. Our lovemaking will become more masculine as the night wears on.

'When we drink together I will stroke the back of your hair because you ask me to, a friendly animal gesture, not my usual style. We'll talk about food a great deal, but won't eat a morsel.

'Whatever, I approach The Magician.'

She returned home with wine. A shoe had rubbed skin from her heel; she took it off to examine her foot, a stripe of blood marked her skin resembling molten heroin running down a piece of silver foil. She walked unevenly, one foot bare, one shod, into the kitchen. She did not see what was actually before her; she saw the fascinating eyes of her Magician.

'I look into your eyes but see only myself. I am not looking at your physical self; I look for the way you want to describe yourself to me.

'I see pain behind your eyes, in the place you want my intelligence to be. I don't want to be there, I want to go on a shopping spree!

No, I don't mean that. The rhyme came easily and I couldn't resist it. I take it back. What I wanted to say was: I want to go forward within my destiny at speed. Faster than the speed of time, jubilantly casting off debris like a roman candle spitting gold into shade number 46 of the 53 shades of black.'

Est removed her stone coloured trench coat and poured a glass of wine. Claudia, her daughter, was having supper with a friend that evening. Est craved roller coaster like stimulation.

'An indescribable beauty I expect, yet will come as a complete surprise in the form of you. I am counting the days until we meet although I don't know when that will be. I have dreamt of you and your life many times, I wait for the time to come when we shall meet. Then I will put on a dress especially for the occasion and be logical and sober.

'And now I think of you. I want to communicate with you, get through to you.'

1.5   Dreamy

In her dream Est walked towards a distant southern city, sunlit and surrounded by sand. A city where extreme virtue and vice cohabited. City playhouse of kings and magi governed by an exotic goddess, super intelligent and extra-perceptive.

A nightmare split the surface of her dream. Her sister confessed she'd had sex with Est's friend Maltby three times in the past week while travelling back and forth from her job in Paris.

'But you can't have,' Est whined in her nightmare.

'It was fantastic,' her sister asserted.

'I thought he loved me,' she moaned again.

'You have absolutely no idea about the love between a man and a woman, that was why he came to me; you simply repress and restrict.'

The pain of incident past and present flowed tidal through Est's sleeping body. In her dream she ran into heathland woods, distraught. She tore at her clothes and her heart boomed as she ran away from her sister's betrayal. 'I really must,' she said to herself, 'be a horrible person for all this to happen to me.'

Est tried to wake up but an image of The Magician with his consort beckoned her mind. Half asleep, she watched as Lillian the Animal and The Magician drank much cognac and invoked Pan. This was not successful as, to put it bluntly, the lingam would not oblige, so they switched deities, ditched Pan and invoked Bacchus. They performed a dancing debauch and Est observed the materialisation of a filament of power, mauve light entwined with silver. As the energy form twisted out beyond the confines of the room into earth and sky, Animal became sinuously at one with it. They danced and sparks of light penetrated their hearts and energised their souls until The Magician fell on to the divan in his studio, drunk and exhausted. The studio Est visited in dreams where he lived with his consort, his Scarlet Woman, Lillian the Animal, in ideological splendour and domestic squalor.

The fine muscles twitched upon the sweating face of The Magician as Animal watched him in his fitful addict's sleep and they, in their turn, were watched by Est.

Images of the magickal couple faded from Est's dream and a pastel pink continuum of sand appeared, stretching along a coastline. A slur of moody green sea menaced the horizon. Pieces of mother of pearl and pink shell glinted alongside whole shells worn sea smooth.

Her dream moved on to a textile warehouse where rolls of fabric were piled one upon the other. She walked past roll upon roll of black silk, each one different from the last. Here was raw silk, here taffeta and here moiré. She felt each between thumb and index finger. She found a door with a green exit sign alight above it; she opened it and found herself in the simple land where sand was made pink by rose quartz, where all she wanted to forget was easily forgotten.

1.6   Peek at Beast

Drummond hadn't eaten for four days; he declared he had no mundane need to appease his appetite. Rather, he said, his ordinary animal appetite had been subordinated to such extent it barely existed. He had learnt the secret of nothingness and was in perpetual association with his holy guardian angel, Aiwaz.

He went out city rambling, wandering where his angel would lead him, he said. But his intellect served a different master, that powerful overlord of the body, heroin. Yes, the crude poppy seducer ruled him and consequently his rambles routinely ended whoring in an attractive admixture of legs and liquid. About which he felt smitten by the spears of conscience not one jot. He put all his whoring down to a wilful whim, only important so far as it assisted his divinely inspired system of sexmagick. His Magician's erotic impulse had to be explored and satisfied to facilitate communication with his holy guardian angel.

He returned to Animal, his Scarlet Woman, once mundanely named Lillian. Once she had combed and brushed her hair prior to routinely leaving her family home at a regular hour each morning. Days off had also occurred predictably. Now Beast returned to her, with fast beating heart, to frenziedly dictate a grimoire, his writing inspired by occult lore and promiscuity. He relaxed his active mind by staring for hours at his Scarlet Woman's yoni, her legs splayed as he gazed upon the pleats and folds of her female flower.

His cupboards were filled with strange items, clothes for one. He thought this luxurious array of lurid garments the perfect Magician's garb. However, here was the clothing of an hedonistic eccentric. His behaviour was unashamedly that of the alpha male, a label he truly deserved. If emotion ruffled self-opinion there was always the heaven of annihilating powders to restore his artificial equilibrium.

Animal was no one until she met him. He transformed her from a half formed limp creature into a noble being of determination and lust. He blew purpose into her, gave a point to her existence far from the preoccupations of the teacher she had in all dissatisfaction been, before that fateful meeting with Drummond, The Beast 666. She became his Scarlet Woman 156, from the fertile land of the Old Testament which flourished and bloomed in the valleys and plains of Drummond's imagination. Animal's ego was invented for her and simultaneously snatched from her by The Beast. She loved to see ego pass before her eyes to occupy the lumpy form of He who never tired of sex. The procession of Self - a new and invigorating sensation, proof that she existed beyond family and schoolroom. But with The Beast stirred and embodied there is no such state as safe.

1.7 Animal Magic

Lillian the Animal was wholly taken up with magick: elemental power and the flow of energy. She was a creature of magick, for her personality had indulged itself in a long long sleep. When occasionally her personality awoke, Animal twisted and writhed with discomfort and she became succubus, nightmare creature living in limbo. She preferred to be an adjunct of The Beast.

Every Saturday her red dress grew shabbier and her behaviour coarsened. Her tongue slipped carelessly around syllables and she showed no consideration to her listener. She wrote to her mother for money. Mother sent her some but Animal did not buy a new dress; she bought café drinks and poisons for her Master. For his temper! For a day's peace of mind and a day's piece of magick. To renew his faith in the potency of his magick, to restore his virility, for his magick depended upon a stiff phallus. Flaccidity told him nothing, transmitted no message from Aiwaz, his holy guardian angel.

Mother sent Animal money and it eased her pain, though it did not improve her wardrobe. She wrote again and asked for more. Mother sent more. Beast was happy, Animal was happy. She wrote again and again. Each time the sums sent were smaller and the accompanying note more worried. Animal told her mother nothing; she simply puffed on her Master's pipe as he mounted her and they performed a magickal operation to summon the perfect mystic musician. She was thin, wasted and badly dressed. All she had left to live for were the possibilities inferred by magick.

Was it for this, one dress and a stump of candle in a chipped saucer, tea without milk or sugar, that she had given up a normal life? No, it was for The Beast and his captivating magick.

She had relinquished comfort for meaning, her humanity for wild passion. She was no more Lillian but the entity 'Animal' and would feed upon poison, as it suited her and her Beast. Of ordinary food, she wanted only the tiniest morsel. All pleasure and sense of unison came from Beast's magick. She rejected her body and was magicko-anorexic, free and at one with the ether.

Chapter 2

2.1   First Meeting With Stritch

As Est drove she became part of the night. Along the country road she watched triangles of deep emerald sky appear and disappear between branches in ever changing pattern. 'Am I the infinite female?' she asked herself passionately. 'Formless until some man, some series of branches, arranges me in triangles?' A man, a magician, whose presence in her life tarot cards had insisted upon.

She was on her way to her parents' house. Claudia, her daughter, was staying with their friend Maltby. Her mother had Alzheimer's and it had made her aggressive. Father had reacted by retreating into books. Est imagined living in a windmill with fields all around and two shiny cars parked outside. It would be close to the sea and the salt air would inspire her search for the man at the heart of her mystery.

Est pictured her mother in her bedroom folding knickers, counting how many were, respectively black, white and champagne. Imaginary mother said 'champagne' and smacked her lips, savouring the decadent word. Then she folded her T-shirts and stacked them in a neat pile. Meanwhile, father told himself that his wife was doing her paperwork upstairs. He had a book open on his lap. He thought with slow sadness, about the passage of time.

'Windmill near the sea. Hand woven rugs.' Est soothed away the distressing images of her parents and associated feelings of injustice. She felt less inclined to visit them. She wanted space and exhilaration to inspire vast canvases of organic colour.

She arrived at a river. Night glowed in oily rainbow colours. Moonlight hung around trees, highlighting their silhouettes as branches waved back and forth. She decelerated before the bridge. Her heart beat with the memory of a night of torrential rain and a similar stone bridge.

She turned the ignition off and engine warmth suffused the silent vehicle. She peered through the windscreen and wiped off condensation. She recalled that stormy night, in a heavy gold car with Claudia's father. They had zigzagged up an isolated mountain road, windscreen wipers inadequate against the driving rain, Est five months pregnant. Climbing the steep pass, he'd failed to anticipate a corner and turned the steering wheel sharply at the last moment; the wheels had slipped and she'd thought, 'If I die, I die.' The bumper crunched into a stone bridge. The headlamps went out. He had joked nervously as he skipped out of the car to check the headlamps. One had come out of its socket; he pushed it back in and miraculously, both lights had come on - no disaster. Est lived, Claudia lived.

The next morning, in their holiday cottage, Est had dreamt that the sea came through the bedroom window. She watched as salt water surged through the five bar gate towards her. The sea was turquoise and alive with octopi and seaweed. Claudia's father had pressed his face against the windowpane until its glass dissolved and he had been pulled into the undertow.

She had parked on a patch of grass by the bridge that had prompted her memory. She listened intently through nature's superficial irregularity, the call of an owl, wind rustling branches and the ebb and flow of running water, to a curiously human hum. The sound seemed to be coming from an alder tree by the riverbank.

A man crouched beside the alder; he hummed as he laconically tossed a pebble into the burbling water. Full of expectation she concealed her presence. Carefully, she made her way to the tree, approaching from the side opposite to his recumbent form. He sat with knees bent gazing at the river; he turned his dark haired head toward Est. His gesture implied the hesitant curiosity of an acutely wounded ultra sensitive person. He had long tapering fingers. His dark eyes were sunk into his head and further shadowed by a straggly fringe.

As he looked at her a thrill ignited Est's spine. 'His eyes are fearless because lifeless,' she noted to herself and felt fate's fingers touch her. For a moment her hair rose up from her scalp; 'Ghost,' she thought and very much wanted to smoke. He didn't say a word as he looked at her with unmoving and unmoved eyes, too satiated to react to fresh impression. He turned back to look upon the river, resting his outstretched arm upon his knee.

'Have you a cigarette by any chance?' she asked as if she'd driven all this way to smoke with him. He handed her a packet of tobacco. She rolled a cigarette and sucked it hard making her bottom lip sore, her throat hot and her ears vibrate. He'd stopped humming. She put the damp fag out on a rock. He passed Est a spliff she hadn't realised he was smoking, in a gesture heavy with emotional backlog.

They smoked in shared silence. The air was still, the road empty. She had left one of the hire car's indicators clicking on/off, on/ off, its spasmodic light created a teasing shadow across his eyes. He pulled a flask from his pocket and sipped whisky, revealing nails studded with chips of black nail varnish. The backs of his hands were as smooth and hairless as a teenage girl's. Lasciviously, Est watched the hump of his wrist bone move as he drank. He passed her the flask and as she drank she tried to summon up whatever it took to speak at a time when nature herself rested and listened to messages from another galaxy.

Est really wanted to make love with him that very moment, in spite of petty reservations. Her throat beat with emotion. She ground her fag butt into the damp leaf mould under the tree and wanted another straight away. He passed her tobacco and laughed lightly, his ironic tone brought her down and she was reminded of her dire bank balance. Coming down, being broke mattered.

She thought of her daughter, with a pang of tenderness, safe with Maltby. Remembered the parents she was on the way to, she ought to have moved on, but dallied here feeling free. And here he was. Coming up from her personal agenda she expected him to have vanished, a personal fantasy, but he had not. He was more real than anyone she had met before in the bundle of haphazard events that was her life.

She played with the idea of tearing away from him, running up the riverbank to the knoll behind, but her most insistent want was for their eyes to meet.

'You cannot see beyond yourself, for all you loved was taken away from you; it is the same for me,' he said and their minds telepathically fused.

He tossed another pebble into the river. 'I care too much about what I look like.' He turned his head, heavy with conclusions, to face Est. Their eyes met.

'I know,' she said, suddenly chatty; 'there are some days when I can't go out because I can't get myself to look right.'

He turned away from her; he didn't want her to be sympathetic, didn't want her to be a woman. She didn't want to be sympathetic, didn't want to be a woman.

'I liked shopping and shagging and caring what I looked like,' he replied. 'But only as an idea.' He spoke only a tiny part of a long train of thought. He struggled for words to describe a precious conclusion he had deliberately isolated himself from society to reach.

Est struggled with desire to shag him. Struggled against the urge to reduce her complex psycho-emotional reaction to him to the animal urge to copulate. 'I don't want to smoke,' she told herself. 'I don't want to drink and I don't want to shag. I suppose he is in danger and he is my danger.' The pallor of his skin and his white hip hugging jeans sent erotic shivers across the back of her neck and down the outside of her arms. She hugged herself and her teeth chattered. She noticed that one of his white knees was grass stained. Another proof that he was more than fantasy. She needed this proof; needed to be reminded that he was real.

Her spine shook as she spoke from the heart in the Celtic fashion. 'Is all I had to offer him was unconditional love.'

'I knew stagnant love, it was all unconditional. And yearning,' he replied empathetically.

'If the body is not benefited by the direction of the dialogue, can world, I mean these words have a function? Should we not communicate solely in pictograms? Is art a function? Necessary not only for cultural satisfaction and sensual ease but our very survival?'

He took a brown medicine bottle with a childproof cap from his pocket. He shook it to show her it was empty and returned it to his pocket.

'What is your name?' she asked, a syllable of it on the bottle's label sparking her curiosity. She had a fleeting fantasy that he was Richie David, missing rock god.

'My name?' he asked with a little smile. He liked the ordinariness of the question, it made him feel he could be anywhere, on set of Coronation Street even.

Est nodded; yes she wanted to know his name; she never not for one moment, thought him a ghost.

'My name is Stritch.' He spoke carefully and his open lips revealed his teeth by the light of the waxing half moon in Scorpio, but showed nothing of his purple tongue.

'Stritch,' she said, earnest as a Jean Cocteau film. 'Stritch,' she confided, 'I love a man I've never met whose name I don't even know. He draws me to him. I thought at first you were a ghost he'd sent to torment me.'

Stritch smiled the ultra self-conscious smile of one who smiled only to maximise the drama of his cheekbones, of one who didn't eat solely to sculpt his face in fleshless contours.

'I know he doesn't love me,' she continued. 'Can't love me. He uses women as ritual tools for his magickal acts to overthrow the Christian Republic. He cares only for power.'

Stritch stretched his legs, stretched his palms against thighs. His lips played with a cigarette before he lit it. 'I have found what you are looking for.'

She was hurt at his assumption of superiority. She wanted to be the most important person under the moon. He was more interested in smoking than in her!

'What have you found?' she asked, stressfully staccato.

He looked at her with his abysmally dark eyes.

'I have found all manner of lies.' He ran a hand through his hair as if to let the lies out of his mind. 'Everyone lies to everyone else and the more they lie the more powerful they become.'

Est giggled delightedly. 'Boring big ideas by liars and cheats.'

Stritch beckoned her to him and whispered, 'I live with an old hag in a shack in that wood.'

'Is she The Magician?' Est asked more as an item in a multiple-choice questionnaire than with any conviction that this hag was The Magician.

'Your magician?' Their heads were one against the other. His hair smelt of acorns, radishes and ginger.

'No! She has a cunt.' The word issued from his throat like the sudden withdrawal of a knife. 'A cunt,' he repeated, a knife flung, 'but she isn't sexy. She is a hag.'

He turned his head owlishly to kiss a liquorice kiss, with a black poison tongue. Her lips were afraid but she was as horny as a nymphomaniac on speed and relaxed as the moment of heroin intake. She responded to his kiss, reptile to reptile. She smelt of the rank stench of distilled passion, needs accumulated through hundreds of years of frustrated bitch ancestors. Her mouth begged him not to understand her until tomorrow when she'd leave him with everything he ever wanted, the surest way she knew to make him never want her again.

'Stritch,' she said as their lips separated 'are we going to...?' His tongue had become a black message of love inside her mind, salivating all over her perfectly ordered intelligence. And it felt good to her; it surpassed the power of their mutual anxiety and self-consciousness.

His tongue searched for her, not her psychosexual masks and decoys, for her.

'Are we?' she repeated.

He threw back his head, creasing his smooth youth's face, his neck veins full of blood.

In a way she was bored although he was so sexy. Something had stopped inside him; people had done something to him, killed his autonomy. He hadn't risked enough nor rested enough; he'd taken pills instead of waiting for an answer. It had all happened too fast. He was like her, like she'd been before she was a mother anyway. In a way they were getting to know one another, learning to fit together.

'Come on, come to the shack.' He took her hand with boyish enthusiasm.

'Her shack?' Reluctantly.

'She's away. Come on.'

He held her hand and she followed his black and white clad back.

2.2   Through The Wood

Branches crackled underfoot as they ran further into the moon-lit wood, wild with the green talk of trees. His hand was fungi damp and clammy. He had begun to tire but Est was fresh. She thought about the hag and her shack. 'Was she a witch who sought a victim? A victim frightened of the world outside comfort food lullabies of cherry pies and spot triggering tutti-frutti ice cream?'

Est wanted to run forever. Vitality poured through his clammy hand and soaked into her body. His was the touch of a bird, lighter than skeletal. Her hand was a warm orange pulse. He wanted to disappear into Est. She loved the black and white of his world, the absolute polarity of male and female. She was struck again by his youth. As old as the river she ran strong beside him, pushing a branch deftly away from their eyes, union in every breath.

He stopped and leant, panting, against an ash trunk. 'Here.' His stomach sucked into his backbone with each inhalation. He pulled her to him; hardly pulled, more a gesture (all she needed), a suggestion that they come together. They slid down the tree. She could see the whites of his eyes as they sat together with backs against rough bark. His irises were an abysmal space she was falling into.

'Here,' he said.

The urgency in his voice prompted her curiosity which in turn rationalised her mood. She had no interest in blind lust; she asked,

'Why here?'

'Because,' he looked into her eyes with sanity and warmth, she felt blood flooding back into his hand. 'Once we get to the shack you won't want me anymore. And I won't want you.'

'Really?' Est queried.

'It's always been that way before.'

'Before? Here?'

'Not here, in all parts of the world. In American cities. Once he comes...'

'He?' she asked.

'Yes him. You'll meet him. You'll like him.' Stritch laughed. He released her hand as his laugh developed into a wheezing cough and he doubled over. His pitiful frailty fuelled her passion.

He lay still on his side. She rubbed her hands together and made them hot with life, tipped her head back to look at her moon through the tree canopy - dormant and leafless yet. She held her hands up to the moon and brought energy into her hands then held them over his navel, to give him vitality. His vitality was not her gift; it was his right to himself.

She held him in an easy caress. They shivered post-exertion in mutual understanding that they both wanted to die more than they wanted to live. Face to face cheeks against leaves warm breath meeting earth. His eyelashes, hard with mascara, lay against her cheek. She liked the shape of his ear under his tangled black hair. She swallowed his breath. They adjusted their bodies to fit together. Her belly was a bowl of light erupting in a mass of volcanic fire. The earth divulged her mystery through Est's mouth aflame as her lips turned translucent orange. He was the moon, the most complete fantasy she had ever met, her equal.

They waited quietly with entwined finger tips, waited for the numbness succeeding passion to subside.

The wind touched trees; creatures grown used to their presence grew bolder. They could hear the river some way off. Est's ears twitched as when she listened for her daughter Claudia's life signs. She could hear the faint click of the hire car's right hand indicator on/off, on/off; she'd forgotten to switch it off. A reminder of the journey home and a reminder that sound is living memory, hearing a way of remembering self. Remembering herself, she still wanted to be with Stritch.

'What is it?' he asked as bats flew fast above.

Her eyes tried to follow the bats' flight path. 'I love you,' she said, reaching away from sex.

She pulled him close and laid soft kisses upon his jugular vein. 'I wantchu.' She ran a finger down his spine; his skin was easy to find under his shirt. They wriggled out of their clothes. Twigs stuck to their legs. They didn't look, they touched. Her mouth was hot orange like the sun. His mouth was hot like the centre of a compost heap, living decay, the fecundity of death, purple. He was her equal, an angel.

Naked, his skinny whiteness held easily to her bronze muscular fleshiness. His decadent asceticism aroused her as his ex-fruit machine addict fingers found her curves. She responded to him as automatically as an oppositely charged magnet within the context of his heaven on earth. Hot goodness exploded from their mouths in chunks of white heaven and Est clung to his ungodly rhythm.

Stritch hooked his chin over her shoulder and held her shoulders with his jagged finger nails. Their beings were gathered devilish in their navels. They felt no cold. They rose from the ground a little, unholy pure and purely engrossed. In their utter absorption the token sexuality described by society burst out from their consciousnesses, and they were spiritual-sensual with no community to turn to. Mankind's harsh laws and taboos in abeyance, they were humble mating creatures.

'You'll like him better,' Stritch said; 'he's the handsome one.'

She couldn't believe what she was hearing, at a moment like this. Out of the corner of her eye she saw the empty pill bottle lying discarded by an ash root, defiantly rearing its shoulder above the earth. She picked up the bottle and read its label by silvery moonlight. 'Prozac, Richie David.' Was he Richie David or Stritch? He certainly wasn't Liam Gallagher, that's for sure.

He shivered uncontrollably and she rubbed him but he did not rouse from post-orgasmic lull. He seemed to be in some kind of coma. Awkwardly she got up and struggling with his feet, pulled his trousers up to his waist, buttoned his shirt. He didn't react as she moved his limbs this way and that.

'Have I done this?' she asked herself. 'Why did I have sex with him poor boy?' As she looked at him moody dejection crept through her; it looked as if their sexual encounter had gone very wrong for him.

'I've got to get him moving. Did I bring that whisky with me? Yes.' She unscrewed the cap; mud in the screw grooves made it stiff; she tipped a drop upon his lips. He choked; she managed to sit him up, rubbed a second drop of whisky upon his chapped lips, rolled his head gently between her hands. He held his head up and gasped for breath; then as she rubbed his chest he breathed easier and his shivers subsided.

Nervous herself with post-coital trauma, she called his name gently, his breath was still feeble and his ribs rattled through his thin shirt. 'He's exhausted. Lack of food.' She gazed at the starry sky, pushed her hair behind her ear and listened. She could hear the hire car's indicator clicking on and off and river water flowing; they hadn't run far. She looked tenderly at his pathetic body. 'He can't weigh much, I'll carry him.'

Est bent down, thinking of the woman who had found motive power sufficient to overturn a car and rescue her child trapped beneath. A portion of such power Est now called upon as she lifted Stritch across her shoulders, hauling him up into a fireman's lift. He was slight, beyond slim; his pale face already as familiar to her as a famous face from history. History in the making as she dragged her legs wearily one after the other, as consistently rhythmical as she could. The 'tick, tock' of the right hand indicator guided her. She relaxed into exertion and loosed her mind upon favourite themes.

She was hot and steadily sweating as she arrived at the edge of the wood. Happily, there was the river and the car. She balanced Stritch's exhausted body upon her own as she fumbled in her pocket for the car key. The moon was reflected in the car bonnet. 'If only,' she thought, 'he could see the fine quality of my love.'

The lock clicked open, she bent down and slid him into the passenger seat.

2.1   Travelling

Est watched Stritch's aura flicker weakly in purple and magenta. She sat in the driver's seat and closed the door, breathing heavily. With relief she switched off the clicking indicator. Shadows loomed with ill intent, sent here by others' thoughts of her. Naively lost for a moment, she locked the car doors, as if locks could help!

Insanely uprooted trees lunged at the car, humanly rapping on the windows. 'These be strong men surrounding me.' Est quickly deleted this sinister thought. She relaxed her lips and connected with hunger. She'd packed a picnic, but before the comfort of food she had to move from this spot where darkness knew her too well.

Stritch! His eyes were closed, his skin damp and sickly and she loved him more than she had when he'd been afire with desire, his eyes darker than hell. She manoeuvred the car through night-quiet lanes and imagined a lazy lioness behind bars, under cinnamon scented sun. A reek of goat by a dovecote where small white feathers littered cropped grass. A lynx behind a high fence smelt the meat of her. Est fantasised an attack of claw and tooth, with all her fears ultimately banished in the luxury of a hundred endeavours against the sharpened cutlery of a cat predator.

They approached a town in need of petrol. Stritch was slumped forward. Est had fixed the seat belt around him and plugged in its silver clasp. The filling station was deserted except for a solitary employee manning the pay window. What time was it? Hell, what time is love?

With petrol she bought aspirin, coke, crisps. Her footsteps prompted no echo. Mauve filaments of petrol exhaust twisted in yellow clouds of electric light. These edge-of-town places are the middle of nowhere.

Est was relieved to drive away. 'Soon I will be myself enough,' she thought, 'to sort Stritch out; no point fucking with his aura until success is certain.' Her hands caressed the steering wheel. 'Enough money in the bank to pay for petrol and confectionary, no more. What are we going to eat this week? Something. I mustn't worry about that. Here we are.' She pulled up on a hard standing where in daytime, outsized farm vehicles turned.

She hurried to revive Stritch with sugar. She fizzed open the coke and poured a few drops into his mouth. He sneezed. 'Excellent,' she approved quietly. She gave him more. He coughed and then swallowed. She reached into the back seat for a woolly rug to wrap around him, turned the car radio on softly and bird mother fed him coke, mouth to mouth. Mutely he accepted her ministrations.

She was tired but didn't have far to go. She had abandoned the original intention of visiting her parents. It was too late to pick up Claudia; she'd have to wait until a reasonable morning hour. She hoped Stritch was in a logical condition by then, whatever that meant.

She drove northeast; the road curved around wind slaughtered oaks. Through the country every 15 miles was a deserted lamp-lit small town. A market square with traffic lights changing to control an empty road. 'As pointless as I am myself,' she connected.

Country again, low hedgerows, high hedgerows, white lines, 55 miles per hour. She was soothed by the soporific effect of revolving wheels. She drank coke for the minor buzz of caffeine. Stritch's arms were crossed over his tummy. He breathed evenly, sleeping in a contented curl. Est worried about him; she was taking him along with her but didn't know where he wanted to go. At least Maltby would be cool about her unusual passenger.

She pressed 'play' on the stereo. 'It could all just be in your mind' in duet with the friction of tyre on asphalt. She imagined losing control of the steering wheel as a tyre burst in an explosion of black rubber.

The music took her mind from a fantasy blowout. 'When I saw the deep distance of your face, we were intimate.' Stritch stirred and stretched his legs, bound by the seat belt. 'She feeds her past,' he muttered.

They stopped at a red light by the old butter market. 'Nearly there. We'll have to stop and waste some time eating until Maltby and Claudia are up,' she explained, more for her own benefit than his.

'She lives in a shack surrounded by trees.' With closed eyes Stritch spoke of his hag. 'She says she doesn't want anything, anyone, but me.' He opened his eyes. 'She wants me so much. She says she's been looking for me all her life. She says she's kind and wants me to stay with her forever. She says, "Relax, I will take care of you, drink Mama Shag's medicine." '

Est pictured a crystal studded copper cup steaming with unchristian chemical reactions.

'She collects herbs from pastures and hills,' continued Stritch. 'She has an ancient pestle and mortar inscribed with symbols of power. She grinds herbs and roots every night.' He held an imaginary bowl cradled with his left arm and worked vigorously with his right. 'And as she pulverises she speaks to me: "I remembered your eyes from my dreams, I knew you before we met. Drink this, love," she says; "drink up all your medicine, it will do you good." '

Stritch looked at Est intensely. 'And now you! What do you want of me?'

She stalled, 'Me?'

He nodded. 'What do you want of me?'

'I want to know about Mama Shag,' Est, guardedly.

'That's not me!' Stritch, distressed.

'When I met you I was looking for someone else.'

'Who's that?' Stritch sulked.

'I don't know his name. I can feel him and every move he makes in here and here.' She took a hand from the wheel and thumped first her heart and then her forehead. 'He wants something alive inside me. I can't articulate; it isn't words he wants from me.'

'I know this music,' interrupted Stritch. He scratched his nose. 'I'll tell you about Mama Shag.'

Down a convenient lane Est came to standstill by a series of hazy dawn lit fields. Flat expanse made beautiful by gentle undulations. In lowlands a small incline has the ambience of a mountain and above the big sky goes on forever.

Salt breeze shoved clouds aside and birds chirruped dawn. With sunrise trees came into their own; seaweed shaped hawthorn trees twisting away from the prevailing wind.

Est clicked off her seat belt and reached into the back seat for the rush picnic basket to prepare breakfast. She pictured an owl, nocturnal eyes peaceful with meat satiety. Stritch spoke of Mama Shag. 'She says she gets her power from not caring if she dies; I don't believe her. I believe she wants to live forever and gets her power from me. I met her only after I'd lost my need for new experience; I was soft and over confident and it was easy for her to take me away from myself. I hardly eat; her medicine sustains me; my own is used up.'

Est recalled the empty Prozac bottle.

He ate the croissant she handed him with healthy enough appetite, Est noticed and was drinking cream rich coffee.

'She never looks at the food she eats,' Stritch continued. 'Food is mystical to her; she eats in silent expression of love for her deity, for her deity is silence. She never speaks directly of her life but when she eats her eyes glaze over and she reveals herself.

'When I was first with her she'd eat raw carrots and parsnips. That changed as she began to enjoy my body and she wanted children's food. I toasted crumpets for her on a fire in her shack. She'd eat them at speed, butter and honey dripping down her chin.

'She could get through crumpets, she could! The first packet I bought, she counted each one she ate. I said to her, "You don't have to count." Apparently she and her husband, now dead, had always counted their food out, how much they were allowed, two crumpets each, or three. I let her eat the packet! She lost count in sticky honey and thick fat, washing it down with a tankard of cocoa. She'd smack her lips and belch.

'She'd fall asleep before she finished the second packet. I didn't feel like eating. I liked to watch her sleep.'

Est smiled sweetly victorious - he'd eaten with her. 7.30 a.m. she noticed, still too early to pick up Claudia. The tape clicked to an end.

Stritch shrank, mouth slack, his power supply exhausted.

'Medicine time,' he muttered as he huddled up and a slow cold shiver set in. Sun was bright upon flat field and curved hedgerow. Est longed to be home; Claudia would have woken Maltby by now. Maternally, she fastened the black belt around Stritch and shifted into gear.

She pictured the owl again as she drove, with purposeful talons and the remnant of a leather shackle around its ankle. She was hyper-aware of her dishevelled prince beside her, he who'd been ferreting for innocence on the insides of too many teenage cunts. His hair was full of bits of the wood. 'Trembling sex frenzy! I could be 56; he could be my son!' Under lycra her bones were icicles though her muscles flexed.

'Too many, too much,' Stritch sleepily.

'Yes I know,' Est agreed, 'teenage fans. Dress like you, walk like you, kiss like you. Want to be you, want to buy you.'

The child-parent bond tugged on her guiltily; she had not done her duty by her mother and father. This made her angry with them. 'Puritan moralistic sexually pure parents. Life's all a lie to them unless it fits with the requirements of their rigid law. Far more than a code of conduct are morals in their lives. Where once there was instinct there is only law.' Thus she justified her impulse not to see her parents. She wanted a genie to deliver the memory of a visit to her parents, Claudia to be delivered to her in the self same genie arms. Genie made of smoky blue flesh, strong arms crossed upon his chest as he manifested wearing king's white shoes. Wise genie from across the routine boundaries of time, guardian of blue infinity.

There to the west were the Priory ruins, their curtain of summer foliage drawn aside. Low winter sun pierced the morning mist and lit the edifice in soft ice cream colours backed by sky in five of the 672 shades of grey observable in a Norfolk skyscape. The prior's ghost still preached to his friars in veiled words meaning, 'Do not be sodomites, do not seduce the peasant girls and do not be drunk. Do not have private lives.' The mown grass around the ruins as neat as the prior wished the morals and priorities of his friars.

The space had such time stopping majesty, that even at 55 m.p.h. it took a stretched while to pass Castle Acre by. The priory ruins stuck up in awkward lumps like condiments upon a table. Then came the ruined castle, a large soup tureen: the past pouring out of its semi-circular remains towards Est, feeding her imagination with ghouls: mind's creatures hoarded from the past. She wanted the sensations but not the facts; she wanted the blue genie smelling of gunpowder, blue and out of the blue; genie in white king's shoes. Not the reality of the lover who slept beside her.

She picked Claudia up more or less at ten o'clock. Felt more guilt that she hadn't visited her parents; she would phone and apologise when she got home. Right now she had to get back and return the hire car.

In Maltby's kitchen, nervously she talked continuously hoping he wouldn't notice the body in the car. She'd backed the car up the run-up so Stritch, snoring in the passenger seat, was on the side away from the house and less visible. To her relief Maltby was obviously tired and not talkative or alert.

Est and Claudia were mighty pleased to see one another. 'Have you had a good time?' asked Est as she escorted Claudia, her backpack and wet wellies out through the kitchen, taking easy leave of Maltby. 'I've got a great tape I want you to listen to in the car.' Est's heart beat as she repeated to herself an oversimplified explanation of Stritch's presence for Claudia. But to her surprise, horror and relief he wasn't in the car; neither was there any trace of him in the lane.

Maltby and Est exchanged goodbye waves. It's important to generate ordinary behaviours at times of chaos. She drove around the village.

'Est, what are we doing, where are we going? Aren't we going home?' wondered Claudia. She always called her mother 'Est'. 'I'm looking for somebody.'

'Who's that? Who are you looking for? Is it someone I know?'

'Where can he be?'

'Who is it Est? Who is it?'

'A boy I met while you were away.'

'Can I meet him? Would I like him?'

'He doesn't talk much and I don't think he's had much experience with children.'

'I don't think I'd like him very much.'

Stritch had vanished. Either he'd hitched a lift or fallen into a ditch, but what could she do about it?

'Shall I play you the tape I mentioned?'

'Go on. Go on.'

'This isn't the right tape.'

'Leave it on, leave it on.'

'Do you have to say everything twice?'

'It's Maltby, he doesn't hear what I say.'

'You're not with him now; you're with me.'

'I've got used to him.'

'What is this?' Est was disconcerted as the tape played: 'I'm going back to Mama Shag. It's my day tomorrow; I know what will happen if I'm not there. I won't let it happen. She can't do without me. I don't know who you are. This happens to me all the time when I try to get away from Mama; she brings me back, she calls me. She's calling me.' Tape broke to the song Est had played. 'It could all just be in your mind.'

'Was that him on the tape?' asked Claudia.

'Yes that was him,' Est answered resignedly.

'Do you like him alot?'

'Yes I do. And I want to meet his friend. He said his friend is nicer.'

'Is that the friend he's talking about?'

'No. Not her.'

'Who was she then? Was it his Mama?'

'No, not his Mama.'

'Who then?' Claudia pursued.

'I don't really know.'

'Yes you do,' she knew her mother well.

'I don't.'

'You do.'

'Come on. Let's listen to the music or you tell me what you did in the country.'

'I want to listen to the music.' Claudia somewhat petulant.

The lyric: 'When I saw the deep distance of your face, we were intimate.'

'Do you like it?' asked Est.

'I like it.'

'Good.'

'I can't actually remember what we did,' Claudia yawned.

'You're tired. You'll remember tomorrow.'

'I'm not tired.'

'Alright, you're not tired.'

Claudia curled her legs up sleepily.

The 45 minute drive back to the city was uneventful. Est encouraged Claudia down the stairs to their basement flat. She turned the key in the lock and pushed the front door open against accumulated post.

They spent a quiet day chatting, eating and snoozing. But when night came and Claudia was tucked up tight kissed goodnight, Est became active. She became obsessive as she padded around the flat. Compulsively thinking through the behavioural equation designed to affect a meeting with The Magician. Their magick to be completed in fork lightning love. It's a scenario of flowers man, flowers and yoghurt, fruit and flowing robes.

She took out her playing cards and laid out a hand of patience and another and another and on and on she played 'cept this was not a game. She was analysing fate through layout subtleties. What did the cards mean?

She could see a bomb; it was out of control. Not because the Great White President would let them have it. Nor because of the revengeful anger of hungry ex-Soviet nuclear scientists, but because the bomb was herself. It was her fear of realising the grace of her nature through The Magician. Yet still she had to seek him out. Where was he? Beyond the boundaries of time? Her mind wandered: when was time not time? When it was in Est's head? When was a skirt not a skirt? When it hobbled? When were shoes not shoes? When they crippled? When was a leg not a leg? When it was in callipers?

Est managed to leave the cards alone at last, to relax in bed with an obscene book then lights out. She dreamt she walked into a newsagent and was overawed by the charisma of the black shopkeeper. While she paid for a newspaper and confectionary his sensual lips mesmerised her. He was a smart dresser in his black suit, white shirt. She kissed his lips in 100% attraction distraction and her dream deepened.

In a dungeon jam-full of prisoners she walked through filmy gauze veils woven in shades of mauve. These veils were all that separated one cell from another. As her body moved, gauze swayed and drifted through space, but not a prisoner moved to escape through the filmy boundaries imprisoning them.

She could hear excited effete voices. Soon she arrived at an open space, stage set in white, where naked prisoners seated at circular tea tables, perfumed themselves and complained mildly about the sweet cakes set out before them on floral china.

Est moved through the veils towards the river Styx, viscous with the blood of a million urban vampires; each had had a hand in breaking her heart.

Claudia dreamt too; her dreams were further away from surface consciousness, more secret, the link between purpose and psyche not yet severed by experience.

Chapter 3

3.1   Animal and Beast

'Animal.' Short, an order.

'Yes Beast.' Eyes meekly to the floor, away from the crimson portrait Beast had painted of her which hung on the wall behind.

'Not Beast.' He was short of breath.

'Yes Master.'

He shook his head and fiddled with his pipe. Clumsily he put it on a side table inlaid with a mother of pearl pentacle and picked up a bumper of claret, left over from the night before. Some ritual or other. He shook his head in half remembrance of the clarity, the black and white brilliance of his rituals when he had still been a man of fortune.

'Lord.' He handed Animal the claret; she drank it down acquiescently. It was Beast's Will and 'Beast's Will must be done,' she thought with a mind as clumsy as his body. They were the dysfunctional halves of a perfectly ordered whole and were both, in their awkwardness, reminded of this. Having drunk claret, traces of humanity flickered in her eyes.

'Drummond, I don't remember anything about last night. What happened? I don't even remember the brief.'

'No matter, child.' No humanity in his voice. 'No matter. Do not trouble yourself with that which does not directly concern you 'Beast' will suffice since it is that word that readily comes to your tongue. Last night, Animal, my dear child.' As he came up close to the young(ish) woman with skin stretched tight across irregular features, he stumbled on a rug. He looked into her eyes with slow heat, one secret of his sexual success. 'Last night you achieved a zenith of abandon; I am pleased.'

Her cheeks flushed pink. Drummond lifted the hem of her

faded paisley skirt with right sun finger and thumb, finger adorned with the most enormous garnet set in silver, replacing the ruby in gold he'd recently pawned.

There was a strained look in his eyes as he lifted her thin bottom off the sofa and watched her face shine in delight. He brought his mouth to suck upon her orifices, not to give her pleasure but to excite her to wild sexual self-expression. His pointed tongue slid into her, played with her, until her womb turned rhythmic. Feeling her response he pulled away smacking his lips. Deftly he adjusted his pink silk cuffs.

'I will be away for a few months.' Briskly.

'What shall I do without you?' she gasped romantic novel style.

'Do not question my decision, Animal.'

'I am not, but what shall I do?'

'You can do your secretarial work. Organise my papers; there are certainly enough words of genius to keep you occupied.'

'How long exactly? How long will you be gone?'

'And next you will ask me where I am going!' Drummond eyed the woman indulgently. 'When will you learn that curiosity can but distract you from the task at hand?'

She trembled violently from head to foot, partly in sexual frustration - she was used to that; he always called short the morning tonguing session as orgasm gathered momentum, never let her climax. To keep her aroused for evening ritual, longing for it. Alive for the moment the magick of the 93 current would course freely through her. He was inspired by her eager devotion.

He adjusted his pink cuffs and called, 'Time for evening ritual, do you not think my dear Animal? Would you like to know who we have visiting today?' Now she trembled in shock at his imminent departure. He possessed her mind and body utterly. They had lived together for six intense months. It encompassed a lifetime of emotion. She saw no one from her previous life. She felt completely changed, although her Master said she had not reached total embodiment of Scarlet Woman, was yet Animal, secretary.

'No Animal. This is your test. You will stay here and continue my Work. Your ability to do so is your task. I must go to a far away place. You have not been chosen to accompany me. This was made clear by the signs I received during ritual last night.'

The evening ritual had lasted long into the night, she remembered that much. Remembered too that she had said, 'No, I won't allow it. I will not.' A man, face shaded by a monkish hood had manifested. Real or imagined? It was always hard to tell during evening ritual. Real or imagined that her yellow robe had been torn at the waist and pulled to one side to bare breasts, that milk had poured from rosy nipples and cascaded over her belly? Panting, thirsty, she had been tempted to drink her own milk. She had turned her head from side to side moaning semi-articulately, 'No, I will not allow it.'

The hooded creature had bent forward and his ice cold fingers had teased her teats. 'I will not allow it,' she had said.

Was she now to be punished for saying 'no' during a dream visitation, punished for asserting her Will?

'Yes you are now to be punished,' Drummond confirmed.

'How..?' she stammered.

He chucked her under the chin paternally.

'My dear Animal, your thoughts are transparent to your Lord and Master.' Animal, who once had been ordinary Lillian, bowed her head in submission. Her heart beat wildly while her mind clung to a part of him she might be able to experience before he left.

'Would you..?'

'You want me to strip you naked, throw you onto the bed from where you watch while I unbutton my trousers to reveal a colossal tumescence which bursts forth bubbling with love juice. Grunting like a base ape I fall upon you and bite your fair white neck, almost brutally, knowing exactly how much to hurt you, while my rough clawed paws...' He held up his white hand and showed her his long manicured nails, the nails she tended. 'open your nether lips briefly before the urgency of my lingam enters your red tomb, final frontier of your femininity.

'Is this what you want Animal?'

She nodded her assent.

'Not that Animal, but you may kneel before me.' Eagerly she obeyed and unbuttoned his trouser fly, her mouth slowly begun to fill. He withdrew before climax.

'Enough Animal, enough. You may attend to me after my morning defecation which I now leave you to accomplish. He clucked her under the chin again. 'My secretary, my Animal.'

*   *   *

Although Drummond, The Beast's departure from their Paris ménage had come as unexpectedly to Animal as monsoon in a temperate clime, he had in fact been preparing for this journey for some time. I say *he'd* been preparing for a journey, rather he'd instructed his other (male) secretary, Pet, to make all ready.

Animal, of course, knew Pet. The two had lived together when Drummond had first arrived from America with Animal. And there Pet had been, sitting in his cage with his tongue hanging out eager as eager can be for such a twosome as Animal and Beast to make such a threesome as Animal, Beast and Pet.

Initially his name had been deFaustian but that hadn't lasted. Initially too he'd courted Animal and they had married. But domestic liason had not lasted either, although sexual association between the two had been frequent under the auspices of Beast's evening rituals. That neither lucky youngster (young in comparison to Beast at least), happened to remember much of their naked and intimate moments can be excused when it is understood they were novices, as yet undeveloped in the art of harvesting initiated self from sensual abandon.

Money to travel had been donated by a certain Miss Jane. Well, it had come through her, via the ritual for attracting subsidy for performing the ritual of manifestation. It had worked a treat. The very next morning Miss Jane had called round, arriving at the critical point of the usual morning ritual sucking of Animal's genitals. Miss Jane had been impressed by the performance, delighted to witness a genuine sexmagick ritual and had coughed up with uncharacteristic generosity in anticipation of what evening ritual might do for her. The notorious candlelit sessions to which outsiders were not invited.

All had been made ready and Pet and Drummond were on their way to an energy laden place of great extremes of temperature, where there was a crack between time tracks. Drummond had spent hours pouring over gematria to establish the exact location. It came finally with Miss Jane. She carried with her the series of symbols that led Drummond to establish, without doubt, the correct location to repeat the 'reverse' ritual at least 1,236 times to charge the holy sphere of flickering white light with his unique initiated presence.

'It is interesting,' Drummond thought to himself as he strolled down the Rue de Boulevard Raspail, 'the less capital I command the faster I reach the goals of initiation.'

He gave his garnet ring an excited twist. His pink silk shoulders shivered a touch; the autumn air was cool after the stuffy red room. He walked with a spring in his stride despite the two, three or so (who's counting when motive is holy truth), bottles of good claret he'd drunk last night. It was a freedom and a relief to be moving forward on his right path. The *I Ching* had reassured him with hexagram No.35, progress. Progress of the highest calibre, progress of the soul. He smoothed a nervous tic from his left eyebrow. 'It is right,' he reiterated, 'Animal must learn independence; to remove the prop of my ego is the most efficient method to assist her on her path.'

In spite of these wise words he was still a man. He could not yet see solely with eyes of power. In his mind's eye he pictured Animal, as he'd left her, sobbing upon the sofa. Her thin ageing skin taught on her bones, her face haggard from their hard life of decadent revelry.

'Solitude will teach her.' This was the last thought Drummond spared for abandoned Animal until his next ritualistic need of her arose. Indeed it would not be for some time. He was embarking upon a series of rituals with a man, Pet, who he was certain had sufficient stamina to bear the necessary repetition of the "reverse" sexmagickal ritual.

Drummond felt his lingam stir within the expensive stuff of his English wool trousers as his thoughts rambled upon Pet's orifices. A heady sensation of freedom washed Beast's senses clean, contrasting favourably with the slow difficult sensations he'd been experiencing lately during morning ritual with Animal. He feared she was becoming domestically attached.

He strode into the café, where Pet awaited him, with a hearty stiffy. A good omen for the beginning of what he was confident would become, in due time, a famous expedition. He was funded, fecund and frolicsome, a fun combination. He hoped Pet had a complementary good omen, in an erect lingam, to share.

3.2   Beast and deFaustian

Light steam rose from two cups on yellow melamine. A mirror on the stain smeared wall behind reflected Drummond. He threw down his maroon velvet hat upon a chair, enthusiasm burning in every gesture.

'DeFaustian my dear fellow, how goes it with you on this fair and auspicious morn?' He noticed the coffee hot and ready for him and was pleased to see that deFaustian waited at his Master's convenience.

'My dear fellow, all set?' Beast's hearty words belied a more intimate sub text as his puffy white paw, sweating cold with glee, covered deFaustian's thin brown claw set with warts and irregular sproutings of hair. Beast looked into his friend's pale brown eyes and deFaustian's pupils expanded with excitement as he beheld his Lord, envoy from the empire of holy spirits. More than a father or Master to him. Yea! More even than a lover. DeFaustian had given his all in ritual and awoken from ceremonial illusion initiate to the blessing of True Will.

DeFaustian pulled upon his Turkish cigarette and shuffled uncomfortably on the hard chair. In spite of deep inner certainty about this charismatic man, this Beast, he was ever a one to express the slightest doubt, to clutch it and dwell upon it. 'You have decided not to bring,' he sniffed, 'Animal.'

'It is to be The Beast and his familiar this trip. The omens are with us.' Beast squeezed deFaustian's hand.

'I am glad of good fortune for our project, but how will Animal manage, in a practical sense, without us?'

'Last night it was proved...'

'Yes, last night.' DeFaustian's eyes flickered girlishly; last night had been a new experience.

'Last night.' Drummond's rich musical voice evoked a protective cavern, safer than a womb. 'Last night we discovered that Animal needs solitude to prove her power and unleash her talent.'

'But Drummond,' deFaustian leant forward in a bird like gesture, 'she is my wife, it is my duty to protect her, to take care of her.' He puffed upon his cigarette; it shrank and wrinkled with the intensity of his suck.

'And it is my duty,' Drummond leant back and his fleshy stomach protruded, 'to ensure her spiritual development. She is one of my people. As you are. A voluntary condition.'

'Of course,' agreed deFaustian. 'But she is vulnerable.'

'Vulnerability is no guarantee of collapse.'

'Then you admit there is a possibility...'

'It is integral to the process. If she breaks down I do not think it will be damaging, all in all.'

'She has no one.' DeFaustian snatched his hand from under his Master's and scratched the side of his Arabic nose.

Drummond majestically took Pet's vacant hand. 'She has us, my dear boy. The work we are to do is as vital to her spirit as it is to yours and mine. Relax my boy, this enterprise is well starred. The first ritual we shall perform shall be one to protect her. Something noble, very noble indeed.'

'Indeed.' DeFaustian raised an eyebrow mentally remarking Drummond's pretty mouth. It wasn't hard for him to relax for he too had noted a perfect set of omens for this trip. Not the least of which was the huge wad of money from that wench Jane.

'And what are you two brewing up might I ask?' A curly haired pouting fellow with the reddest lips, drunkenly set himself down in a third chair. 'A night of passion?'

'Passion for a purpose,' Drummond replied coldly, aware that this man considered himself the superior poet in present company.

'The purpose of passion is ejaculation. Ecstasy perhaps?' Mahoney called for a bottle of vin ordinaire and glasses. His companions refused the hospitality. Mahoney shrugged and slobbered as he continued, 'And the purpose of ejaculation is impregnation? What are you two huddled up here looking fecund about? I might say pregnant with meaning?'

'To be fecund is a state of being,' Drummond replied icily, enjoying the ice. He was half ice half foment. He knew that to be put down is a good start for rising to new heights. Mahoney's arrival was another good omen. Drummond mentally slotted him in as a functionary part of his Great Work.

'This is the stuff I like to hear.' Mahoney drained another glass of red plonk, his face twisted at its vinegariness. Drummond enjoyed watching Mahoney's distaste; he rubbed a knee against deFaustian's under the table.

'Yes the stuff from which sublime experience is made,' continued

Mahoney. 'I could do with some of that. When are you going to invite me to one of your famous evening sessions?'

'Fame is a condition from which I eternally seek escape.'

'Running away from Paris and your good friends are you?' asked Mahoney in his lush Celtic brogue.

'Running away? I think not. Escaping? Certainly not. Leaving Paris? Perhaps,' Drummond replied complacently.

DeFaustian ordered more coffee.

'I heard all about last night. Can't wait to get a chance at it myself.'

Drummond took a piece of notepaper from his pocket and with a fine resin and gold monogrammed fountain pen wrote an address in a sophisticated script He added a series of symbols beneath the address.

'Take this Mahoney. At eight o'clock tonight my alter ego will wait on you.'

DeFaustian looked sharply at Drummond, recognising the address as his marital home wherein dwelt Animal. Drummond nodded sagely.

'Will you be there then?' persisted Mahoney.

'Who is to say where I'll be or who I am?' Drummond stood and arranged his hat stylishly in the mirror. 'It is not who that matters nor where; it is purpose - intention. Look for three symbols, omens if you will, before you knock upon that door at eight o'clock tonight. Look for fire, a broken ring and the colour orange ubiquitously applied. Come Pet; we must depart.'

'Fire, broken ring, orange,' repeated Mahoney.

'The ubiquitous colour orange,' corrected Drummond from the door of the cafe.

'What do you mean by that, man?' Mahoney, scarlet cheeked.

'I mean be sober and observant and you will be rewarded with discovery. I think you are poet enough to accomplish a reasonable interpretation, as the symbols are revealed.'

'Poet enough, you're right there, I am that. Thank you and bon voyage. Whatever it is you're up to, bring me back a stick of rock.'

Mahoney in his long greasy overcoat and absurd squashed hat, was yet bohemian poet enough to be elegant and attractive. He waved briefly to the disappearing backs of deFaustian and Drummond.

'Are you going to warn Animal?' deFaustian asked his Master, perennially cautious.

'She will know what to do.' Their steps made a rhythmic tattoo. 'I rather like him,' Drummond decided. 'I think he'll do well.'

DeFaustian passed an anxious hand over his brow and checked his watch, thinking deliberately of the boat rather than his wife.

Mahoney watched the contrasting figures of Drummond and deFaustian, as they proceeded down the Boulevard Raspail at fast pace. DeFaustian with short staccato stride while Drummond was gracefully athletic. From behind, the great Magician appeared quite slender; he carried his stomach in front with pride, as one would a favourite sycophant. The two men turned a corner; Mahoney observed deFaustian's reptilian hand gestures as he was displayed briefly in profile before the pair disappeared from view.

Mahoney blinked a few times and rubbed his eyes, sore from the effort of observation. All he wanted for himself was contained in the energy emanating from those two men. The very air around them throbbed with animal magnetism.

Mahoney shook his messy russet curls. His hand absentmindedly upon the glazed door he moved to re-enter the café, but was momentarily stalled by a man in a navy suit and hat coming out. This interruption of automatic behaviour woke Mahoney sufficiently for him to recall the piece of paper with an address upon it that Beast had given him. 'Not evening yet,' he thought. 'Won't get drunk and recite poetry, not today, won't drink.'

He read the address. It was close by, hardly more than a few strides. Clouds moved from the face of the sun and bright rays pierced Mahoney's sore eyes. He blinked. 'Enlightenment, indeed illumination. Fire, an omen,' he murmured in the bass rumble of his poetic inner voice. He stalked off in the direction of the Animal, Lillian deFaustian, sex secretary to the Beast, worker for inner freedom.

Mahoney walked with rolling gait as if one leg were shorter than the other, although this was not in fact the case. His was the walk of the ancient mariner, of one whose lifetime had been spent metaphorically all at sea, and now but half alive searched the land for the harmony of the sea.

*   *   *

When, but a short hour ago, Beast had left Animal alone with the devastating news of his journey, she sat for a while silent and cold upon the edge of the red sofa. A sofa which in more auspicious moments doubled as a copulating couch. Her hands twirled and thumbs pressed hard together, as if by channelling blood to that patch she'd find a reply to inner need. Her need to feel sure about something, anything within herself, on her own terms.

But she was dependent on her Beast; without him she was vegetable matter, an untended pot plant wilting on a windowsill. Beast had even introduced her to her husband! And where was he? She knew deFaustian loved her and cared about her in an ordinary way; but she was also aware that what they mainly shared was total loyalty to Beast. Away from her, her husband could only be with him, slave to Beast. Their marriage was an extension of Beast's Will, a facet of Beast's sacred destiny. Pet's care for her, his attachment to her soft hair and sweet kisses, was easily overridden by Beast's demands.

'His needs! His needs!' She stood up, alert and ready to flee, then deflated she sat down, he had commanded her to stay. His needs! All that had been done to her body in the many exotic names of his needs! She'd done it for magick and for knowledge. Her head drooped and she sat awhile, absolutely still, empty and bereft. She sat as Beast had often bid her, without consciousness of any personal needs, awaiting instructions. Waiting for inspiration and the sense of *his* purpose, her Beast's intention to enter into her.

Chapter 4

4.1 Hello Stritch

Nothing came between Est and the night, no opportunity or desire. She sat on the floor of her unlit flat nervously, while dreams sped through her head. The spectre of a white clad girl appeared in the kitchen doorway, sorrowful and knowing.

Est warmed with love memories of Stritch, remembered his charismatic disappearance. Mad thoughts of obsessive love charged up her spine. Red arrows exploded in her mind insisting, 'Go go go'. Then a fractionally cooler energy entered her mouth. Her lips blossomed and she quivered with the excitement that was Stritch; that was their liaison. She wanted to find him and be with him. She adored his creation of himself as a piece of power endowed nature rather than a pathetic human thing.

Stritch smelt of a bigger *he*, the *he* whom Est searched for. Stritch had imbibed The Magician's elixir of life; Est had tasted it when she'd licked his skin.

'It could be a maternal impulse I have to reach out to him,' Est considered. 'Possibly, I'm reaching out for another child and Stritch in the same movement of heart. That sounds worse than simply a maternal feeling. Sounds like I want his baby. I haven't come all this way on my own taking enormous artistic leaps, to be reduced to the banal bimbo sexism of 'I want his baby.' I've known girls who talk like that, but now the girls seem different; I don't know.'

*　　*　　*

'Hello Stritch!' He was back at last, on the phone. It had been a while. Where had he been? How was he?

'I went back to Mama Shag, Est.'

His voice was carrion bird rough. 'What has she done to him?' Est wondered. 'What has he allowed to be done to him?' She envisaged Mama Shag's isolated damp cellar where a few tough old hens roosted, clucking amidst the reek of chicken shit. Stritch scene centre in white jeans hanging loose from his waist, stud button undone revealing a puckered navel and limber waist. His head hung to one side, his black shirt erotically ripped. A new red bite on his neck with bruising around neat teeth marks. Mama Shag hovered around him, her face a huge Long John Silver ham of a visage.

'Are you there now?' Est spoke into the receiver. Her voice comforting and alluring, as if she's expecting a parcel and he's the parcel.

'I'm on my way to you. I passed the bridge. I thought you might be there.' He sounded young and vulnerable, a cliché of sex appeal.

'Waiting for you?' She dropped her voice a tone or two.

'Yeah waiting for me.' Slowly articulated.

'For five weeks?'

'Is it that long?' He'd obviously been on one.

'At least. It'll be good to see you Stritch.'

'I'm coming now... soon.'

'Do you know where I am? You've never been here.'

But he'd hung up.

Est spent one hot minute in an agony of jealousy. She imagined Mama Shag in that basement splashed with hardened chicken shit. Mama Shag was spanking clean and her eyes sparkled with health. She was not a woman of words when her sex passion ran high. Nor a woman to be taken in with the minor league stimulus of sense impressions; she barely looked at the gorgeous young man, though her green eyes were on fire. There was a sacred place from whence came her desire, a heaven she'd invented for herself and drawn Stritch into. He the fallen angel? Est shuddered and rummaged in her lingerie drawer where, in a small red basketwear cylinder she kept a crystal. It was easy to find and cold as ice. It was frosted grey at its base turning black at its tip. She tried the pointed tip with her thumb; it felt good.

She faced south and wondered how much Stritch and his connection to Mama Shag had to do with her search for The Magician and the fulfilling relationship she longed for. Wondered how much of god there was in the whole business and how much of the devil. As her mind steadied yogically and the crystal warmed, she felt a directional pull in the energy lines of her left hand. At this most inconvenient time, the front door bell rung. She wished she were living in an isolated windmill.

'It's probably not even for me,' Est speculated, 'but for next door; they never hear the door.' She fondled the crystal in her hand, longing for Stritch. She thought she'd try her door, just on the off chance. She opened it and there he was.

'Stritch! Come in.' He smiled at her sheepishly. 'How come you got here so fast?' she asked

'Fast?' As if he didn't know the meaning of the word.

'Yes, you only rang minutes ago.'

'Minutes?'

'Well, half an hour.'

'Half an hour?' He didn't seem to know what half an hour was either. They entered the flat; it had felt warm but now was cold. A mauve astral cloud gathered where she'd stood holding the quartz. Stritch walked straight into the cloud, opened his mouth and sucked it in, closing his mouth up afterwards, in the manner of a genii returning to its bottle. He glowed lightning mauve, a figure cut out of a clever as fuck movie starring an anorexic Johnny Depp.

Est felt foolish asking a fellow who'd recently swallowed an astral cloud:

'Would you like a cup of tea?'

'Yeah, why not?' He turned to face her, stared through her and his body crumpled up. She thought he was fainting, but no, it was his way of sitting down. Once seated he was cheerful. 'Where's that cup of tea then?' He lit a cigarette and she brought him an ashtray.

'Shall we drink this?' He produced a bottle of okay red wine she hadn't noticed him carrying.

'Yes,' she replied, 'let's drink that.'

4.2   Animal and Mahoney

Mahoney, poet, drunk, romancer, stumbled up the steps to the apartment where Lillian lay mute upon a chintz sofa. She was an empty muse, a wooden leg of a creature without her Master to fill her with sacred fire.

Well that was what he told her he filled her with. Spunk (sacred fire), wine (sacred fire), cocaine (sacred fire), opium+heroine (sacred fire), hashish (sacred fire). More wine more spunk and a journey to a long low building in Scotland where the wind crooned an eerie ballad for all those who dared stand by the lightning tree and listen. The locals said that that was what drove Drummond's pretty young missus, Irene, insane. She'd wrap her arms around the stricken trunk and sing with the wind. Maybe she'd lost herself in the wind or maybe it had been the oriental variety of sex positions her husband practiced that stole her sanity.

But we were talking of Mahoney, not of Drummond's first wife. Mahoney stumbled up the stairs to Beast's Paris apartment, muttering, 'Ritual, ritual, damned unholy ritual. What did I hear about his damned unholy ritual? Lord only knows.'

He rapped on No.32's battered door. He leant against the doorjamb, arm raised up to cushion his head. His dun coloured raincoat hung tattily from his form, as a piece of sacking from a scarecrow. The ends of two short legs stuck out underneath. His trousers had frayed turnups folded over hobnailed boots. Fresh animal odour oozed from him after his stair climb. Waiting by the door Mahoney got comfy, so comfy after morning wine, that he nodded off into a snoring snooze.

Animal was not roused from her melancholy by Mahoney's heavy rap; it was the vibration of his snores that penetrated her desolation. She put her ear to the door and decided this snoring hum was exactly what it in fact was, a friendly snore, and opened the door. Mahoney fell, his prop being removed, and was thus startled into wakefulness. The tipsy poet removed an imaginary hat, (he'd actually left it in the café where he'd happily squandered the small royalty cheque which had arrived that morning), and bowed.

'Mahoney at your service Madam.'

'Madam?' queried Lillian the Animal.

'Miss Lillian I come from your esteemed Master, Drummond, with whom I have had the fine fortune of meeting this perfect day.'

'You've seen him?' Lillian reached for Mahoney's arm and pulled him into the apartment. This news and the soft kindness in his light brown eyes were enough to access her trust.

'Please sit down, Mr...?' Animal smoothed her dress in an habitual gesture and offered him the maroon sofa, a sofa used to the moisture of human juices.

'Thank you, so kind. Mahoney I am called. Poet, wanderer, cavalier. I mean that not in the sense that Casanova was a chevalier, but maybe in the sense that Lancelot was, or that Mahoney will be remembered for so being.'

Animal passed him a glass of red wine she'd noticed him glance at with hungry dog eyes.

'Did Drummond send you?' she asked eager for news of He whom she adored. Greedily our poet knocked back the wine complete with dust film and dead fly. His head instantaneously relaxed, chin fell to breastbone and he slept, as drunks will. He snored, still holding the glass.

Animal sighed. This turn of events, this visitor at least would occupy her. 'He seems to be one of us,' she thought. 'If he wakes in time I will be able to observe our usual evening ritual. Drummond said it would be so. The Beast always delivers.' With such thoughts she sat lightly upon a Queen Ann reproduction chair and lifted her flowered frock above the line of her stocking tops. Her fingers passed under the loose leg of her lace edged French knickers to laconically find the folds of her sex.

She lifted her knees until her feet rested on the chair cushion; her wafer thin body fitted easily into the chair. She reached for her carved wooden phallus, stained dark with sex juice and pushed its smooth outsized head into her yoni. Her head flopped sideways. A yellow tit threw itself with a thump, onto the windowpane and twittered confusedly. Animal pressed the phallus deeper into her yoni, a yoni trained to respond sexmagickally morning noon and night. All night.

She panted and sighed. The chaotic rhythm of her breath awoke Mahoney. He opened his eyes and in amazement dropped the crystal glass, (one of four and worth a few bob. Drummond still had fine things casually about him). Mahoney's eyes had opened upon slim stockinged thighs apart. Shaved pubis baby bare. Dildo vanishing into swollen vulva lips in the broad light of day, birds twittering. 'This is what they get up to,' he thought to himself. He was erect, eager and fascinated, upon his knees kissing her thighs, pressing them further apart, biting her thighs kissing her nude sex, tickling her with his shaggy curls. She groaned, not caring for a while that Drummond had gone.

Mahoney, ordinary man that he was, was romantically inclined, in spite of circumstances suggesting a different female inclination. He tenderly removed the wooden phallus, now strewn with mucous, deeply sniffed the smell of it, holding it to his face, tasting it. Lifted her in his strong arms to a low divan, really a mattress on the floor, in a shadowy corner. Laid her limp acquiescent body upon the soft stained cushions and fiddled with his trouser fly to release himself. ' Blessed saints be praised and forgive my desires, my lusts; bless my lust,' he rambled. Animal meanwhile, was a long way off inside herself. Mahoney's erection was released, hard and proud as any girl could wish for after a long night of party-party. Then a knock came upon the door.

Trancelike Lillian sat up, the glazed look of sex unfocussing her eyes.

'It is he,' she said mesmerically, 'he is come.' She walked to the door, dress lying where it would. It was indeed he. The Beast. He looked ten times the man of any other; his eyes glowed with sacred fire; he wore his clothes subtly in ceremonial style. His forehead bore memory lines of a thousand and one orgiastic nights.

'It is I.' In he walked, deFaustian scampered after him. 'I need my sacred horn of plenty.' Simply put, he had forgotten his cocaine and his heroin.

Beast more than filled the room, the tentacles of his nourished Will reached into every corner and beyond, through the walls into the street. Mahoney was both embarrassed and in awe.

'It is you,' Beast addressed Mahoney. No words came from Mahoney's open mouth. A minute before he had been on the very verge of falling in love with a lovely girl, romantic sensibilities astir. Faced with her husband on the one hand and her Master on the other, he was lost.

'Take him into the bedroom. See to his needs. Quickly,' Beast ordered deFaustian.

Beetle-like, deFaustian took the big poet's hand and led him into the bedroom. 'We must do as he says,' pleaded deFaustian's eyes. Neither man spoke. DeFaustian gently closed the door to the dingy windowless bedroom holding Mahoney's bewildered eyes with his own. DeFaustian tidily undid his trousers, pulled those and his pants down to his ankles, knelt down before the low bed and offered Mahoney his arse. Mahoney was rooted to the spot, fear strengthening his erection. DeFaustian looked round at him again with the pleading look that said, 'We must obey.' Mahoney moved not.

The Beast threw the door open.

'Good.' His body filled the doorframe. His presence was a tidal wave replacing the stale air of indecision with the sure perfume of his intention.

'Good, proceed,' he commanded Mahoney. He flicked up the tails of Pet's jacket with a cane he carried to fully bare the small arse; it was covered with half healed welts.

Mahoney moved not. He held his trousers up trying to hide his aroused prick. Beast's gaze bored into the poet. His command was more drug than drug could ever be, for his authority had within it a human element, controlled and irresistible. Mahoney bent over the form, slim as she he was destined to love. The Beast prodded Pet's anus with his stick, opening it. With great sensitivity, he pushed the stick in then withdrew it. The brown anal creases responded flower like. Despite his revulsion, Mahoney bent over Pet. His large heterosexual prick bubbling liberally with pre-come, went deep and immediate into Pet's arse, surprisingly wide once inside. Mahoney felt great relief, though he did not feel quite himself. He pushed with rampant thrusts and a feeling of love in his heart.

Pet exchanged a sly grin with Drummond. Animal crouched at Beast's feet and licked his ankles. As Mahoney's face creased in ecstatic tension the Beast brought his cane once, hard down upon the fleshy freckled buttocks. Mahoney cried out in painful ecstasy. Beast produced a hypodermic syringe and injected the poet's buttock with heroin. Mahoney's orgasm came from a place he did not know existed prior to this strange day. He was simultaneously sick.

Beast carefully stowed his drug filled horns and wrapped his voluminous crimson cloak about him.

'Take care of him my dear,' he instructed Animal as he left her for the second time that day. 'You must complete him tonight. This evening, no less.' She nodded.

DeFaustian took Drummond's arm as Animal watched as they strode rapidly down the street. Two gentlemen together.

4.3   Est Needs Freedom

Est needed movement and freedom, needed to feel her heart burst out from all known definitions of love. Love! Love for Stritch. How could this stretching at the pegs of her edges, distorting her personality into crazy grimaces, how could all this amoebic emotion be for a him? A him alone, a him here now?

Stritch, there with her in her city flat. She loved the way he lived far away from civilisation inside himself, wherever he happened to be. His body crouched over hers waited to fall into her, to thread her personality through with his creative tension, his mushroom madness, his genius, his lost soul.

The curtains were open and the room was lit by the diffused light of one angular street lamp. Stritch buried his tousled head into the pit of Est's shoulder. He smelt through her soap, perfume and fresh skin oil, breathed the deepness of her. He fell in a vertiginous descent of knowing her.

They didn't want to have sex with each other this night of the perfect crescent moon. Didn't want to take their clothes off and show weird ghost flesh, were shy as vampires in daylight. They didn't want to shudder, gasp and remember a million life details. They went away from desire to a nameless place and in this nameless place to orgasm. It wasn't a baby-making place. Wasn't a swan monogamy place nor a green dancing place. Not Bacchanalian. It was a place of untried guilt, of guilt enclosed and guarded. A place of imprisonment and a sorrowful journey across the river Styx. A place of white underground creatures knotting around each other sensationless, their bodies breaking and rejoining like maggots enacting scientific explanations of being.

In genderless copulation they blended into one another and were whisked to a godless climax by nerves and blood alone, filling each equally with revulsion and elation. Nausea overwhelmed the need for insurance, assurance. Nor did they need vocally to assert that they were together or separate, exalted or debased. Or that sex was good; they both knew that sex was good; that its grey ugly aspect was unimportant. A grey unimportance like waking up irritable from sleep. An ugly urge forgotten, remembered, express-ed, hidden, providing no access to the genius they both craved. Within him yet not of him, within her yet not of her.

She ran her hands through his thick dark hair picking out dead leaves; bits of twig, an acorn cap. She made a ball of these between her palms, rolling them together along the distinctive line of fate which cut her left hand in two.

Stritch and Est sat, their backs against the sofa, hands loosely joined, hair mingling. They smoke nonchalantly, that mood in which all smoking should occur. The night breathed lightly. A supernatural bird of prey flew to the window, perched on the sill and scanned for supernatural food. Sharp eyes searched, beak pierced Est's neck and it folded its wings and fed on her blood before flying off again.

Est's fingers flickered over Stritch's; she withdrew her hand and twisted her ring.

'And when Mama Shag leaves you in the hut to live again in her spacious country residence, what happens then?'

'Nothing happens.' Stritch laughed and his fingers reaching for hers were like scampering ants setting up a new community. 'She lives according to a boring pattern really, not even a pattern; habits. The habits she had before her husband died and she became a widow. And she keeps those habits religiously! You'd never believe it, she's *so* religious. Then when it all drives her mad and she can't stand another moment of politeness, she goes to her shack. And me.'

'Her shack and you?' repeated Est moronically, fighting guilty feelings of possession and jealousy. She wanted this mangled feeling to go away; it ate into her. She longed to meet her Magician. Stritch was too like her, too wild, talented and knowing. She was afraid and she was a mother and she had to uncover her fear and uncovering it felt like picking a scab that ought to be left to heal. Stritch opened up all her healing wounds. He knew no responsibility and she was afraid.

Stritch continued, 'She falls upon her knees and prays fervently; small stones press painfully into her skin.' He paused to pull upon a cigarette lit from the butt of the last.

'What does she pray for?' encouraged Est, her stomach still orgasm nauseous, doing more listening than her head.

He inhaled before answering, 'She prays for many things.'

'Yes what?'

'You're eager to hear this aren't you?'

'Not really.'

Stritch pressed her hand. 'First she prays that god's, I mean God's holy churches shall always be full of high quality worshippers.'

'I didn't even think she was Anglican; you're winding me up.'

Stritch smiled out of the corner of his lips and blew a few smoke rings. Then hearing a distressed murmur from Claudia's room, Est got up. Stritch tried to hold her down; she pulled away and went to her sleeping child. Claudia was too hot. Heat in the night and her head sweated and she tossed and turned; the covers twisted around her. Est loosened the covers, turning her over as she did so. Claudia sat bolt upright and opened her eyes.

'It's only your Mama, your Mama come to tuck you up and say goodnight.' Claudia settled down, shutting her eyes, still asleep; had never really woken up. Est folded the covers back and opened a window. She returned to Stritch wanting to hear the rest of the story, but the moment had passed. Stritch slept, his body slumped sideways.

'Why does it always have to be incomplete. Why does it always have to be like this?'

Chapter 5

5.1 Drummond The Beast and DeFaustian 'Pet',
Wayward Couple In Transit

Drummond and deFaustian were in high spirits as they set out from gay Paris in transit to the Sahara Desert some 35 years since they'd first met at Trinity College, Cambridge.

Drummond had two marriages behind him, two ambitious mountaineering expeditions, 36 disciples and a mighty tabloid reputation. Women meantime, had become a new species, much to the taste of Drummond. He liked the strident sensuality of new woman and the short skirts. Aroused, he did what came naturally to a gentleman; he took what he wanted. Took a wife, used her up, threw her back to her family. Took another who suffered from jealousy, Her Problem of course. Magick was master of all Beast's emotions. Wife II followed the first; no guilt or regret. In similar enthusiastic vein he had spent his inherited fortune and now lived on his wits, selling oriental carpets and accumulating debt.

Drummond fully deserved his magickal name of The Beast, while deFaustian, in true grinch style, capably embodied his, of Pet.

It was a fair train journey to Marseilles from where they would sail to Algiers and from there be desert bound. The omens were good; indicating that the two gentlemen would be honoured by a mystical event of great import.

After a soothing train journey, sipping whisky and reading a great many newspapers in four different languages, (Drummond, by the by writing an article on cosmic law), we join the adventurers on board ship in the tiny cabin they shared. They were stowing their luggage in the small space beneath the bottom bunk.

'I shall take bottom bunk, my dear.' Drummond, The Beast, announced pompously.

'Why should you choose first? Why shouldn't I have the bottom bunk and the first choice?' De Faustian, Pet, was irritated by an item concerning genetic supremacy in one of his Master's articles he'd been editing.

'Why should you not indeed?' He brought his eyes slowly to deFaustian's, to powerfully texture 'why'.

'I shall have the bottom bunk.' DeFaustian placed his wash bag possessively upon the bedspread.

'Shall you walk before me or after me when we pass through a door?' quizzed Drummond, The Beast.

'What usually happens at doorways?' Interested in the question, wrong footed in the power game.

'When we are alone together?' Beast's sensuous voice was hoarse from smoking.

'Yes, when we are alone together,' deFaustian replied pettishly, pulling at his jacket collar, frayed from previous like attacks.

'When we are alone, I rearrange the matter of my organism and appear to walk through the closed door while you fumble with the handle.' Awash with the scent of vanilla and neroli, Beast took his friend by the shoulders.

'My dearest deFaustian, old friend, familiar. Pet, partner in adventure, apprentice, scholar. My dearest envious one.'

DeFaustian, Pet, regarded his Master's face grown large and flabby with umpteen nights of high excitement; the mouth seemed to swallow him whole, just as Jonah was swallowed. He was humbled as fleshy mauve lips met his own in a mystic/erotic act he had grown used to, the mingling of saliva.

Sensing doubt lingering in Pet's soul, Drummond The Beast took a knife from a hand tooled leather case. He made a small incision in his lower lip, a drop of blood sprang forth and dropped onto his shirt where it merged with the maroon velvet stuff. Who could know what other stains lurked unseen upon that shirt? He held the knife, hilt carved fishlike, up to Pet's lip. Pet pressed his lip against the cold blade and he too bled. He sucked the blood into his mouth and met Beast's lips, their blood commingled. This snake kiss brought forth tumescence in both men.

Beast snapped the blade into its hilt and stowed it. He took a pinch of cocaine from his horn of plenty and rubbed a mite into their lip wounds. He poured a nip of whisky into two beakers. The men clicked glasses, eye holding eye. After drinking they lay upon their bunks to peruse Russian newspapers. Beast upon the bottom bunk, Pet relaxed on top; one leg hung over the edge and rustled the corner of Beast's newspaper.

'I have a letter here from a Mrs Whiter; she says she is among the first of your disciples.' Pet had brought Beast's postbag with them and read to distract attention from the mechanical grindings as the ship's engines stirred to life. Beast, in spite of his proficiency in the Russian language was not sorry to be disturbed.

'I have many such devotees.'

'This Mrs Whiter, have you heard from her before? She complains that "Despite many generous donations, in some instances," she admits, "somewhat beyond my means, I have not yet heard from The Beast. I am sure that this is a simple oversight." '

'Must we hear it?' The Beast lit his hashish stuffed pipe.

'Wait. It will interest you. She continues, "As requested previously, I would dearly like to be initiated into the next level, but know that to progress I need The Beast's saliva." '

'How in heavens did a suburban hausfrau come to that conclusion?' Drummond The Beast rose up from a lazy recline rather suddenly and accidentally dashed his head against the bunk above. Pet's eyes danced with wild forest boy mischief.

'There are suburban hausfraus and suburban hausfraus.'

'I shall hazard a guess. Our Mrs Whitter...'

'Mrs Whiter,' corrected Pet.

'Our Mrs Whiter is a suburban hausfrau.' Beast settled himself comfortably.

'I haven't got to the...'

'The interesting part of a hausfrau's day? Could it be shining saucepans or scalding the front door step?'

'We shall play chess later,' challenged Pet, formerly known as deFaustian.

'Rather I shall beat you at chess later.'

'As it should be. You shall beat me at chess later. Even though you shall beat me, we shall still play and the game will appease your need to be tiresomely witty.'

'Am I tiresome?'

'You my dearest Beast, are the most fascinating fellow. You, an Occidental, have pushed further into the sacred heart of the East than many learned Orientals have themselves.'

Beast, perennially pleased at praise, relaxed and dozed off. His pipe dropped from his lips and a fragment of hot hashish resin fell onto his neck and roused him.

'What about this Mrs Whiter?' A small white blister erupted in the soft vulnerable base of his neck where the resin had touched.

'Her letter continues. "To become a high initiate in your system of magick is now the only concern in my life, since my husband passed away not six months ago. I have a lifelong interest in spiritualism and it was through contact with *the other side* that I became interested in your system. I was contacted one evening by a spirit professing to be an urban vampire, saying my blood would be good for him.

"My companions at the table wanted to be rid of this spirit they felt was malign, but I had no such feeling. On the contrary, I felt I was meeting an old friend, someone I had known for a long time, who I was meeting in my conscious mind for the first time. I know you will understand as you have described such a thing happening to you. This vampire spirit left the table at great speed after two of our company experienced extreme trauma; one was sitting with her hair standing on end and the second had turned grey.

"The same night I had a dream, so vivid it was verging on the real. The vampire came to me, his face covered by the folds of a deep red cloak. I felt peaceful, a peace I had not known since the unhappy demise of Sidney, my late husband.

"The vampire or Beast, as I later came to know him, bent over me and spat upon my neck exactly where the jugular vein lies; then sucked upon me. With great pleasure I felt his tongue working upon my neck, great enough to bring me to a crisis. The next morning I examined my neck and found bruising but no trace of an incision. I looked and felt younger than I had for years though my eyes were a tad bloodshot. Menstruation commenced two days later. I am a woman of 62 who had long since hung up her glad rags!" '

'Yes, yes,' interrupted Beast impatiently, 'standard sexual wish fulfilment. Must we hear more? Come on, let's dine.'

'A moment more. And it concerns dinner.'

'An excellent one, I hope.' The Beast liked to feast on food as well as other varieties of orgy.

'Mrs Whiter continues. "It was upon the third visitation that the vampire revealed himself. As yourself. The Beast 666. You welcomed me to your stable, pronounced my role to be mare to your stallion. I feel such gratitude to have been chosen in this way.

"Where I was lost, I now am found. Where I was old and wizened I am now young and foolish. Where I was once forgotten, discarded (even my family no longer brought their children to visit me), I am now courted. Young men fight for my attention. I never knew such a life was possible. Thank you Beast; thank you for your magick.

"In part repayment for the great gifts you have bestowed upon me I am reading all your works and learning how to be of service to you. To this end I have obeyed your spirit instructions to sail on the same ship as your human form and make myself available to you to use as you see fit.

"I am very nervous, as you can imagine." '

'Good grief who is this woman?'
'Mrs Whiter, I told you. Doris. And we are to dine with her at the Captain's table. Apparently the captain took one look at her and bagged her as a pretty picture.'
'At 62? She must be a remarkable woman.' The Beast dressed rapidly for dinner. With gestural efficiency he removed and folded garments, took his evening wear from his leather case. He understood how to settle his appearance from the inside out, without a mirror. Especially when his imagination thrilled with a novel situation.
'Fun, fun, fun with you about. Let's not forget that chess game.' Pet leapt nimbly from the upper bunk.
'62 years old. Ha ha! What do you think we shall be served at dinner? I am ravenous. Any other crackers where that letter came from? Does she profess a taste in bare footed foreplay beneath a dining table? How do you think she would like most to receive my divine spittle? Shall I propel it to her across the width of the Captain's table? Or should I conceal a blob of digestive liquor in my hand, to press upon hers with a sensual rub?'
'Make sure you have the right lady.'
'Indistinguishable from the virgin filly of 15 we spied in the saloon earlier?'
Pet nodded in reply as he adjusted his tie and collar; greased back his short brown hair. A little grease dripped, unnoticed, onto his collar.
'I would like game pie,' settled Beast turning the handle of their cabin door.
'Game pie with Doris sauce?' quipped Pet.
'Initiation is initiation, duty is duty. The system must be followed.'
The narrow corridor glimmered with polished brass, the change of air from the thick smoke within their cabin sobered them

quickly. Pet felt dizzy.

'Should we leave the cabin door open to air it?' In reply The Beast opened the palm of his hand and sucked. As if by magick, by magick in fact, the heavy hashish smoke spiralled neatly into the palm of his hand and was no more.

'I must rid myself of this on deck,' he muttered as the smart couple entered the splendid art deco dining room, exactly on time.

Chapter 6

6.1   Animal: Scarlet Woman

Animal shivered by the window; Mahoney was a clammy cold presence behind her. 'The Beast is always hot,' she thought devotedly. His instructions rang in her mind, 'Complete him this evening, initiate him.' Mahoney towered over her, big as The Beast. Animal staggered back. He descended upon her with wet mouth. She turned her head and he missed her mouth leaving a trail of drool across her cheek.

She met his eyes with all the meaning of The Beast's consort, The Scarlet Woman. Speckles of black in her hazel irises sparkled in, what Mahoney interpreted, an ethereal fire about to consume his soul. He had read about souls (wrote poetry, you know); had been wondering, in wine and out of wine, if he had a soul.

Mahoney paused as Animal poured strange fire into his heart.

'You may call me Animal.' Her wide slant eyes wrapped right round her head, her fringe curled up to the ceiling.

'Animal, my dearest Lillian.'

'Animal,' she purred.

'Animal, you have ignited my soul and turned my blood to fire.'

'Save your poetry heathen, we must take you to a broader plane than the narrow corridor of literature.'

'We?' stammered Mahoney, big mouth hung open, red cheeks reddened.

'We,' repeated Animal authoritatively; she had a duty to perform, a devotional service.

'?' Mahoney looked askance.

'Simply accept "I" am "we". If you are lucky one day Beast will explain how "I" is "we" in Spain or North Africa. All our emotions serve his soul; he'll make you happy.'

'I will be happy?' He wasn't sure where he was now the affects of his morning wine had worn off.

He didn't remember how he had got to this place nor why he had come here, to a shabby yet fashionable Paris apartment, this one more claustrophobic than most, with its red furnishings and fetid atmosphere. He resorted to his normal ploy when feeling lost: recitation! Of his own poetry! He sat on the lumpy sofa beside Lillian, brushed aside the flap of his dun brown overcoat and took her acquiescent hands in his.

'I am in thrall.
The wild waters of the lake,
Sent me from my homeland.
I was challenged by the silver waves
Of a ripple filled night;

From whence a thousand nymphs came
To tend me.'

And more in such vein, while Animal planned his initiation that very night. He was open and trusting as he squeezed her tapering fingers in his fat freckled ones.

She was at peace now she had embarked on her mission. On a human level she enjoyed this keen young man's company, which made the initiatory process easier for her. She smiled to herself, thinking of his initiation. Mahoney tossed back a curly lock triumphantly, believing she smiled in appreciation of his poem.

For the moment she would be still, outside time, would wait for owl time. 'Later,' she thought, 'I will use the white altar. Marble and glass.' They had to leave this red place with its bloodstains and secret windowless quarters. They would go to *Ridelands* in England with its spring green park, perfectly ordered tree clusters and elegant undulations. She would stand before the bay window in the Ballroom and look out through mellow rain, her vision blurred by water. Not a stranger in sight, just crystal, marble and dishevelled Mahoney.

Mahoney was winding down. 'The erotic enrapture faded/As my grieving heart becoming jaded/Lost innocence with knowing/That outside it was snowing/And she was sending me there/Into the bleak midwinter/Without a care for my welfare/Without love I go.'

'That's your poem?' asked Lillian with a clipped secretarial voice, though her eyes were cat slitted with diabolical plans.

Mahoney was dazed. For better for worse, the bubbling brooks of green Eire and all that, he'd wedded poetry.

Lillian placed her cool left hand over his clasped sweating pair.

'Yes!' He jumped. 'My poem!'

'Your poem,' said Lillian with finality, then: 'Have you a change of clothing?'

'Clothing?' he repeated stupidly.

She nodded. 'Clothes, to put on. We're going on an exciting journey.'

'Clothes? An exciting?' Mahoney garbled.

'Journey. Let me get you a drink. Brandy?'

'Thank you.' Confused, he stood up and removed his aged raincoat, smoothed it over the sofa arm. Lillian poured him a drink.

'Won't you join me?' Mahoney asked remembering himself, attracted anew to Lillian.

'Me? No.' She shook her head, then smiled at him with her wide clown mouth. 'I have an adventure to prepare. Remember?'

Mahoney drained the glass and automatically held it out for a refill. He felt better already. 'Funny,' he thought as he shivered, 'how my body temperature varies.'

'Are you cold?' Lillian asked him, still in a short sleeved cotton dress. She passed him a second tumbler of brandy.

'How did you know?'

She winked. 'You shivered. Lie down,' she indicated the settle in a shadowy corner of the room. 'Relax while I pack. I'll find some of Drummond's trousers for you.'

'Drummond?'

'The Beast. My Master. You've met him, I believe.'

Mahoney shivered convulsively; he couldn't talk through chattering teeth. He staggered over to the settle and pulled a silk throw over his knees. He felt safer in the darkest corner of the room. Twilight oozed through the window. Lillian drew the curtains and lit a black candle held in a distinctive pewter candlestick with a snake coiled about its stem.

When she returned from packing in the adjoining windowless bedroom, Mahoney was in a light trance. His eyes were focussed on the invisible and an earthy odour of fear seeped from his body. Animal's stomach rumbled. She poured herself another brandy, took one of Beast's pipes and filled it with a mixture of tobacco, hashish and opium. Smoking, she was a replica of the insanely grinning figure in the painting on the wall behind her, a portrait of her good self by her Master 666.

Mahoney, rousing, acknowledged the likeness as he took the pipe she offered him. He choked on it.

'What is it?' he gasped, 'I have never...'

'Have you never? Have some more, relax, feel it.'

A natural born trouper, Mahoney renewed his efforts with the pipe and was rewarded by a lovely mellow mood. He felt confident. He passed the pipe to Lillian and made room for her to sit on the settle beside him.

'Lillian my darling,' in sonorous poet's tones, 'you are an extraordinary woman.'

'And I will make your life extraordinary,' she promised.

They nestled together, candlelight flickered over scruffy furnishings. Quietly they finished the pipe and Mahoney's hand subtly slipped down to the hem of Lillian's skirt. His hungry thumb travelled up the silkiness of her stockings to the intensely pleasurable moment when silk turned to flesh. He worked his way across thigh flesh to silk knickers, warm with her blood heat. He drooled as he ran his fingers over the fabric covering her sex, imagining its exotic shape, colour, texture and the taste of her, sweet and sour.

Lillian leant back comfortably, lifting her knees. He felt her through her knickers until her pelvis rocked.

It was relaxing for Lillian to have a humanly sensitive lover after the magickal ravishings she'd experienced in homage to the fabulous lingam of The Beast. She recalled a cavern underground and an acutely sexual compulsion. Recalled a melodic chanting as innate rhythms surged through her body.

Mahoney's fingers were inside her knickers as Lillian thought of Beast's passion. Gradually she ceased to be organised, fastidious Lillian and became unruly Animal.

Mahoney too was transforming, though not losing his humanity for he had not yet been initiated into that specialised way of erotic expression. His sexual impulse was still gender specific and monogamous; that is, he got horny for a woman, his woman.

He pulled her knickers off and buried his nose in her sex. She stretched her legs and using her fingers, displayed her tenderest parts for him to adore. Mahoney kissed her shoulders and neck, fondled her girlish breasts, fumbled to remove her dress as she writhed out of it.

They made strong penetrative love. He stroked her until his hands lost sensation. She hooked her legs around his back to place him exactly where she wanted him and together they found synchronicity. They listened to the beats of one another's animal instinct as they soothed anxiety away.

6.2   Lucky Couple in the Country

A week later, Mahoney and Lillian stood in hard sun on the gravel drive of an elegant English country house, manikins before a dolls' palace. The air was fresh with May mist; damp breeze stirred new formed leaves and a strand of Lillian's hair. She pushed it back behind her ear. Mahoney started as a hallucinatory flash revealed her as a younger woman with strawberry blonde hair and freckles sprinkled over her nose.

Lillian was underdressed and diffident. A gust of wind lifted her blue georgette dress above her knee revealing her stocking top. She stood unabashed; her lack of inhibition alarmed Mahoney anew; he could not understand the motivation behind her sexual behaviour. Sensing his bewilderment Lillian turned her sly sparkling eyes to him and smiled, all lips, cheeks and eyes. She pulled him towards her intention, a secret she held. He gasped for breath and stumbled. His fall was arrested by his shabby cardboard suitcase. He kicked it and it rattled on to the gravel with a sound that sent a bolt of pain through tender molar roots. He clapped his hands to his ears in a silent scream.

'Need a drink?' asked Lillian smirking as she reached down to pick up her hardly less tatty suitcase.

Mahoney communed with the mottled sky, seven shades of grey displayed as vaporous clouds hung heavy. Cloud shapes changed and trees rustled as nature spoke to him in a language he surely, at that moment at least, understood.

'A drink?' Lillian repeated.

'How fine to find myself here,' Mahoney exuded tenderness, 'a place I would not have imagined myself.'

He picked up his case and they strolled towards *Ridelands'* grand white columned entrance.

'Why not?'

'A humble soul like my own, born to river and trees, to be in the midst of such grandeur!'

'Don't you like it?'

'Yes!'

They put their cases down on the doorstep and in a sweet romantic gesture Mahoney took Lillian's freezing fingers in his own freckled paws. Wanted to warm her into the carefree young woman he had seen in sudden insight. He embraced her. 'How good of you to have brought me here.'

'We expect a great deal of you,' Lillian asserted, aloof. She lived not for herself but for a set of instructions she cherished in her mind.

She had to push the brass front doorknob hard to open the heavy door into the musty gloom of a spacious hall.

'The rooms above are light and airy. That's where we shall be. Let's go straight up.'

'Is this your house?'

'Oh no.' With light steps she led him up a narrow side staircase, once, he assumed, used by servants.

'No,' resumed Lillian, as she led him through archway after archway. The air was fresh and perfumed. 'No, I own nothing in this world. *Ridelands* belongs to a higher initiate than I. A true magician.' The beautiful scent grew stronger as they proceeded.

'A magician?' pondered Mahoney.

'Yes. You seek truth don't you?' She stopped before a door adorned with elegant symbols.

'Yes I do,' he answered simply, as he would in a court of law.

'And that's why you came to me?'

'Yes,' he replied, altogether her creature.

'Good. We shall do well together. We will please The Beast.'

'The Beast?' Mahoney again perplexed at this loaded name.

Animal stretched her arms, tipped her head back and made a series of guttural noises from deep within her throat; the door magickally opened before them.

'Drummond,' explained Animal conversationally, picking up her case and entering the room. 'Don't you know he's The Beast you seek?'

'I thought The Beast was within myself.'

'A poet would.' Animal laughed as she sat down with a girlish bounce upon a large brass bed in the middle of the room, the mattress unusually high above the floor.

The room smelt of cinnamon. Light blue sky spilt in from

south facing windows. There in the West Wing, they had entered a warmer world. Animal unbuttoned the first button on her dress. It had buttons all the way down the front. She unbuttoned it to her waist and pulled it down over her shoulders. She lay down upon the bed, her emaciated breasts bare. She wore nothing under her dress but a tattoo - a seven pointed star of Babalon between her breasts, superimposed with a phallus and enclosed within a circle.

Mahoney was wildly excited, but controlled his erotic feelings as they disturbed him. He didn't want to have sex with her under orders of this Drummond The Beast. However, his Will was not his own and a moment later streaming sunlight blinded him with the necessity of burying his head, his eyes, the very essence of sight into her heat.

He knelt in front of her, but the bed was too high to reach the part of her that invaded his senses. Gently, he pushed her further onto the bed, her body glowed otherworldly. The counterpane was soft and attractive, made of thousands of tiny patches. He kissed her lips, but found no softness cushioning her jawbone as her lips were stretched thin and taut as if wrapped around her face. Everything about her made him wilder, even this curious grimace. He didn't need to open her with his fingers. He could find her wet slit easily as, for now, all his intelligence resided in sexual impulse. Little effort was needed before pleasure intensified beyond pain, to a place with no name.

In the tension of orgasm Mahoney slipped out of the known world, into deep sleep. He was exhausted and confused yet still excited and erect. Animal deftly rolled herself out from under him and finished removing her dress. She stood naked before the window, then opened it and climbed through with lithe exuberance, her heart racing playfully. She skilfully climbed down the wall and nimbly jumped the last six feet to land lightly upon the terrace. She turned and ran across the lawn, down the ha-ha and through long meadow grass.

6.3   Country Scene

Twilight came upon the spring evening, upon elegant *Ridelands* and into the room where Mahoney rested, his first deep sleep in the days and nights that had passed since he'd met Animal.

Long slanting shadows of window frames and restless trees danced on the walls.

Mahoney lay uncovered, his limp sex pink-innocent amidst curly auburn hair. Cold, he shivered and sat up, confused at being awoken by sunset.

Lillian had left a note for him pinned to her vacant pillow. 'Gone for a walk, will be back to eat!' He smiled, a leap of ordinary love in his heart. He wanted to overcome the mysteriousness he associated with her pallor and placidity. He wanted to love her in normal homely way and for her to routinely reciprocate.

He looked about for light, though he barely needed it; the room trapped sunset and more light streamed in from an adjoining room. The door between the two rooms had been removed and a rough arch constructed. A curtain of heavy orange brocade hung to one side.

It had been in this bedroom, when he'd first arrived, that he'd removed his travel weary clothes, worn for weeks. His stained Paris trousers had been fit for nothing at all except drinking too much cheap wine in.

Since that time days? weeks? had gone by. Time had passed in the frenzy of bodies' sticky hot togetherness. Now alone, sex satiated, Mahoney stretched and his spine cracked. He was naked, cleansed. He passed through the archway to the adjoining room and experienced a strange tug in his abdomen. He now saw what he had not before, marks etched in the uneven surface of the plaster, Arabic letters admixed with Egyptian hieroglyphics. With his rational eyes he couldn't understand them, but as he looked they came alive, self illuminated and discharged their meaning directly into his mind. A meaning he couldn't articulate; it articulated him! But he did know that to walk through the arch constituted a rite of passage, a journey from which he could never return. But he'd had that feeling many times since he'd met Lillian. 'Why is this different?' he asked himself. 'Because I acknowledge it intellectually?'

Passing through the archway his hair prickled with static. He came to a dressing room equipped with water jug, towel, robe and thick soled slippers. No mirror, which meant he couldn't shave. He washed, surprised at the thick layers of dust, sweat and mucous on his skin. He was shocked at the flabbiness of his buttocks. How long was it since he'd been accurately aware of his body? How bad had his drinking become? How obscene, middle aged and alone was he? He considered these issues as he donned the coarse clothes he found, heavy and abrasive to city skin; no undergarments provided.

The dressing room led on to another room. His steps were slipper silent as he entered the light drenched room. He noticed for the first time since childhood the position of his toes in footwear and made a mental note of the importance of foot welfare.

The third room was a kitchen. There was a large table for preparing food upon and eating around, a stove with a basket of neatly chopped wood beside it. He opened the oven door; inside a fire was ready laid, matches conveniently close by. He lit the fire, obedient to the intention behind the organisation of the kitchen and the prompt in Animal's note - 'will return for food'. Flames moved easily through the calibrated wood. He placed two slightly larger pieces of wood upon the fire; heat flooded his face and a stray flame singed a side lock. He drew back, shut the stove door with a snug clunk and opened the air vent to draw the fire. He knelt and listened to flames roaring through wood and the gush of air rushing up the chimney.

Upon the table was a pewter candelabrum, primed with seven beeswax candles. He lit these as sun's orange rays dwindled. At the window, he reached up to lower the bamboo blinds and upon the lawn below a small figure ran. Lillian! She ran and turned in a lithe dance, her naked body spun up and down. Sensing his presence as humans will, she waved to his framed silhouette, integrating the gesture of greeting into her dance. Then the rising light from the candles erased the scene and all he could see before he finally dropped the blinds, was his own reflection in the dark mirror of window. August and leonine, his hair a mane around his head, his robed body dignified.

His spine trembled at the sight of her. Young man's post coital hunger ravished his body. His stomach rumbled. He was famished and wanted to eat his girl, or rather feed his girl as well as himself. Wouldn't take a bite until he could share it with her.

He whistled, bustling about the kitchen, enjoying the smell of hazel wood burning. He'd let the wood burn well to build up a hot heart, before damping it down to a steady cooking fire.

Miraculously the kitchen was supplied with potatoes, carrots, dried beans. Onions hung entwined and freshly churned butter was wrapped in clean paper and patted with the same seven pointed star symbol he'd feasted his eyes upon between Lillian's breasts.

He put the beans to soak and chopped carrots and onions. He damped down the fire and put the potatoes in the oven to bake. 'They will take a long time to cook through; we shall be ravenous.'

'And drunk,' Lillian added reading his thoughts as she glided, scarlet robed, into the kitchen. 'This wine is very good. Mmm! What are you cooking?' She examined Mahoney's fledgling preparation, pushing back a stray black lock.

'For your delight and delectation a simple broth, fresh and clean upon the palate, stomach filling yet easy on the mind.'

'Why easy on the mind of all things?' laughed Lillian, wielding a corkscrew.

'We are created by the food we eat as much as we are created by our parents and by god.' Mahoney stirred his broth with a dramatic flourish of his wide sleeved gown.

79

The cork popped and Lillian held the claret to her nose; it exuded intoxicating mulberry vapour. 'Am I to be a bean and a carrot today?' She poured wine into two pewter goblets without waiting for the wine to breathe.

'You are, rather, to become what the humble carrot and the simple bean have to teach you.' Mahoney tasted the broth added some salt and stirred.

'I'd rather be taught by grass.' She raised her goblet. 'To transformation and completion! The Cup and The Sword!'

'The Cup and The Sword,' echoed Mahoney, satisfied with the poetry of the toast.

'By suggesting I'd respond well to humble carrot and simple bean, are you insinuating I am usually egotistical?'

'How could I? You who have me in thrall! Oh no, I am simply saying you could eat a little more and not do badly from it.' Slightly embarrassed at having to explain himself.

'I'm too thin am I?' Skeletal Animal drained her goblet.

'Let us eat, most beautiful and revered of women,' extolled Mahoney, tactfully bringing the pan of broth to the table.

'Too thin, too thin.' Lillian poured more wine for herself. 'Since the corset was abandoned and skirts rose, I have heard nothing but "too thin".'

'Let us eat my darling.'

'And later we will make magick.'

At the word 'magick' Mahoney's entire face participated in a wave of anxiety. He drained his goblet which Animal then refilled, along with her own.

They opened a second dust covered bottle of the good wine and for a while ate in silence, hunger kindled by first taste of food. It had been numberless hours since they'd last eaten. The food cheered Mahoney and the wine helped too.

'Tell me woman of mystery, ethereal and lithe sky nymph, from whence came you?'

'Me?' asked Animal, primitive and guttural. 'I came from a sordid slum in London. Yourself?'

'I was born by a babbling Irish brook; green pastures and owl haunted woods were my play places. In the house was poverty; nature was my refuge.'

'My refuge was the whorehouse. In the end,' between bites, 'home was a nightmare so I left; I soon had my own flat. Posh part of town too, that's where I met Drummond The Beast 666. He was my client.'

'And then you fell in love with him?' asked Mahoney, thinking *meat, meat, meat* as he watched her chew.

'It wasn't like that.' With a lingering feline tongue she licked broth juice neatly from her long white fingers. Mahoney entranced, hallucinated that she sucked the flesh from her finger leaving naked bone gleaming in the candlelight.

The candles burnt slowly with an exotic smell he could not quite place, pine and musk, reminiscent of deer in forest, elusive and wild.

'You want me to suck your cock?' she remarked casually, in response to his lascivious expression.

'Your mouth is as wide and tempting as the seven seas upon which I would wish to adventure only aboard a sturdy ship. I refer to a body, my body, currently in ruins. You ravage my reason my dearest. If not love, what attracted you to Drummond The Beast?'

Lillian banged her goblet down, sploshing the ruby fluid. 'The Beast! Money! The excitement of money! The glamour of money! The comfort of money! The adventure of money! At first it was money. In those days The Beast was rich; he bought me and I was glad. I did anything, everything for him for money. Our time together was spent in the dark under belly of humanity. And I didn't care, for where there's sin there's gold and hadn't I, Lillian, Animal been brought up to sin?' She tossed her words into the candles, their aureoles flickering in time with her speech.

'Born to sin. What horrible fate was that?' Mahoney asked in deep sympathy.

'A fate of seduction. I never knew innocence, even as a child. Innocence is a memory I do not share with humanity, therefore I am not a human being; I am an animal.' To demonstrate she got nimbly upon her chair and lifted her skirt to show him her dark haired palace of Venus. She placed her hands in the form of a triangle, thumbs and index fingers touching over her pudenda and then placed this triangle apex upwards, over her forehead. Her scarlet robe rustled back over wiry legs as she maintained this pose for three long seconds before crumpling back into her chair. Silent, emotionally drained. She was a perfect liar, making up a past for herself at her convenience rather than reveal her very ordinary, middle class origins.

Mahoney misunderstood the emotion of her speech. He felt it hopeless whereas she meant it in triumph and celebration of self invention. Masculine and conciliatory, a generous tear fell from the corner of a pale blue eye.

'Why not leave this Beast? Come away with me?'

'Leave The Beast! Come away with you! Why, you are as much his creature as I!'

'Surely not, my dearest,' Mahoney remonstrated gently.

'You are,' she reasserted. 'And surely you would know you are if you tried to walk or think or cry or eat outside his influence, outside his magickal territory.'

'How can you be so certain of this?' He looked into the small puddle of wine remaining in his goblet, dappled with sediment.

Low thump of a cork drawn by Animal from a third bottle.

'I am his woman. Can't you see that? His creature, his Animal and his Scarlet Woman!' They faced each other, breath bated in between the curved arms of the candelabrum. Flame illuminated their faces and formed shadows within the hollows of their eyes; cheeks and chins appeared purple as old bruises.

'His Scarlet Woman. What is this? This Scarlet Woman?'

'I am the Scarlet Woman who rides The Beast of Destiny. I am a lover, I love. But I am only half of truth. Love is the Law, Love

Under Will. A Rider, a Beast and their motion: there is no emotion. I act like a lover upon every occasion; everyone I meet is my lover. I have no formal manners; all my manners, all my actions are the actions of a lover. For I am Lover of The Beast, I am his Scarlet Woman. The Beast is he who can bring us all to completion, to creation, to nirvana. He rebirths us!'

Mahoney's lips parted to accept her words and the life of The Beast. Then suddenly a smell of burning carrot hit his nostrils. He'd put the pan back on the stove and it was burning dry.

'A convenient distraction,' Animal commented lounging in her chair, ankle crossed on thigh, cowboy style.

6.4   They Can't Get Enough

'Look at me.' Their bare bodies close and slippery, creating a jungle climate in the world of bed. They had spent five days and five nights in total mutual flesh indulgence. Lillian held Mahoney's head between her hands. His parched lips compulsively attracted to hers. He didn't know he was hallucinating, didn't know she'd laced the cake with a secret ingredient from her enchantress's arsenal.

'Look at me.'

He was reluctant. 'Lillian, I don't have to open my eyes to see you. I can see you clearly inside my head, all your lovely frightened self. Let me close your eyes for you with my lips; let me close your heart to any love but mine.'

'Not my face. Not my body,' Lillian the Animal remonstrated.

'Your fiery eyes then, they that burn the dross from my ideas, scorch all false love, consume all experience I had before I met you.'

'I am but the vehicle of power. Look at me Mahoney,' she repeated from her position amongst pillows.

'Can't we blow the candles out? It's so bright my eyes hurt. It is as if my eyes are living inside my mind and my mind is the centre of the sun, vividly ablaze with vision and ideas undiscloseable in such scorching splendour. Can't you blow out the candles?'

'Come closer and look at me; see the radiance around us; see how we are illuminated by The Beast's bright psychic rays.'

As a paper book jacket printed with the same design as the hard cover beneath, so synchronously in distant clime, the scene is of the same essence, linked inextricably by energy and ritual. Beast and Pet had reached their desert destination.

Chapter 7

7.1 Desert Ritual

'Into night's womb comes blood, viscous with the vitality of the new killed. I pour blood upon this spot, our eastern pylon.' They had carried a pigeon in a cage across the Sahara desert. Drummond The Beast now held it out in front of his purple and gold robe and slit the bird's belly with a small silver sword. Its blood spilt into a pit in the sand, dug as one vertex of a nine pointed star.

'Before The Beast and his Demon, witness thou Earth, the fecundity with which I invest ye. In return I bid thee invest me with the power, mine by birthright, and the high rank of Magus! Master Therion! And I will do unto ye as ye do unto me. Love is the Law, Love under Will.' Drummond The Beast passed his hands rhythmically before his chest emblazoned with the symbols of his magickal progress, rather as a boy scout is decorated with badges variously awarded for orienteering, rock climbing and chess. These gold braid symbols reflected scraps of moonlight.

In that land of sand and wind stood The Beast, warm pigeon gripped in bloodied hand. Before him upon the ground, squatting over the small puddle of blood fast soaking into sand, was Pet, previously known as deFaustian, naked but for heavy collar and chain. He followed his Master, with a mind as dark and opaque as Mahoney's was bright and transparent in the magickally correspondent green English scene.

Pet's mind was concentrated, not by peyote buttons, but by endeavour, enforced to the point many would call torture. Judge not. There was a purpose and free will was the only power invoked to reach this desolate place of dust.

They had walked, ill equipped, without guide, relying on instinct to find water. Primed by arrogance, supercharged by ritual, the dark side fully manifest in flesh. Robed Beast strode, swathes of white cloth about his head, staff in hand, focussed on a rationally impossible journey he knew could be accomplished. In his hand was the leather loop end of a leash, by which he'd led Pet, who'd crawled naked in the heat, skin burnt to suppurating blisters. Jerked along unmercifully by the man who held the keys to his heaven, Pet had fallen forward unable to keep up; his cracked lips hit burning sand. Sand in his mouth, in his eyes; no water spare to wash the glassy grains out of his eyes. Sand lining his orifices; he'd struggled again and again had fallen. Beast, an impressive billowing form calm and single minded thriving on hardship, had addressed the grovelling Pet.

'Are you finding the journey hard and the going rough?'

Pet had nodded. Gasping in thirst he'd pointed to his dry sand filled mouth.

'I will give you three fluid ounces of mint tea.' Pet had nodded vigorously, as a dog would. 'Enjoy; then I will punish you for your weakness.' Hangdog look from Pet. 'And I hope you shall enjoy your punishment as much as I shall.' Pet nodded keenly. Beast had smiled papally noting the fly on Pet's eyelid suggesting near presence of water.

Pet had taken the flask and drunk in small sips as Beast had indicated. The tea was tepid and sickly sweet. Beast had stowed the pewter flask within the capacious folds of his robes from whence he had taken a strong plaited leather thong. Beast had lifted the lash above his head, his silhouette the dramatic pose of spear wielding hunter, his hunger not for food. He'd thought, 'I will need to bring this lash down hard and accurate to take proper effect.' He'd wanted the sting of the whip to vibrate in Pet's liver, gut and kidneys. Wanted to teach him the nobility of subjection. He had laid two strokes upon Pet's vulnerable midriff; the snake tongue had licked lasciviously. The sun had been at full force and too brilliant; shadows were but small puddles in its near vertical angle.

Beast had shaken his shoulders to relieve the muscular tension of sudden exertion and had blown out through his teeth on to the back of Pet's sun boiled neck as he'd tied his demon's hands tightly behind his back. Pet wouldn't be able to crawl now; he would have to walk.

The Beast had raised his arms into the sky. His indigo robe shared colour with the atmosphere; his stubbled throat was long and lumpy as he'd tilted his head back. Pet had scampered around his ankles whimpering; he'd crawled under the robe licking his Master's salty ankles.

'Begone!' Beast had roared. Pet's body had trembled, his arms clung tightly to his master's hairy ankles.

'Begone!' Beast had roared again and the sound travelled out into space. With no material surface to receive the call neither 'be' nor 'gone' had echoed; softly the words had diffused around the two men. Then sunset approached, wind had stirred ice chill upon the undulating rolls of sand forms like an infinite plane of frigid femininity.

'Begone!' Beast had called a third time. The wind came up; Beast felt the wind of triumph rise through the many folds of his white headdress (fastened with a cornelian) and his face had relaxed.

Pet's whimpers had risen to higher pitch and he'd curled his sun burnt limbs around his Beast's legs. Pet's sinewy body had quivered with the passion of subjection. His eyes had been shut tight, his breath drew in Beast's stench.

Wind had turned around magician and familiar until their sense impressions had died, overwhelmed by the moment's vitality; initiation had been upon them. The time had come to pour fresh blood into the sand; the pigeon would serve its purpose.

*   *   *

The morning after the pigeon ritual Pet awakened in stifling African desert heat. He lay within his Master's robe, his head right up against his Master's arse. He squeaked piggish, unhappy after a strained sleep; his night's rest had resembled the stress of a wheel in perpetual motion, held temporarily still.

Pet's burnt body jerked and his head squirmed towards light and air. The effect of which was to head-butt Beast in the butt. This woke Master who hated to be woken mid dream, the continuity of his subconscious disturbed.

Beast bellowed and set into a frantic wriggle to extricate himself. After some exertion the two men realised their relative situations and disentangled themselves.

Pet knelt before his Master and kissed his feet. Beast grunted as he kicked him away.

Beast, hot and tumescent, staggered forward and beckoned his companion to morning ejaculation ritual. Pet scrambled to his feet eager to serve his Master sexually with his pointed tongue, keen to collect his Master's sacred seminal fluid for magickal purpose. Pet's snake-like tongue teased grunting Beast's lingam and quickly finished the ritual to hold within his mouth the sacred juice. That morning it was highly concentrated, intensely salty. He savoured the unique personality of its flavour and texture as it slowly slid down his throat. Pet sent prayers to Pan as he swallowed Beast's spunk.

Beast leapt up nimbly, ten years younger; the triumph of the previous night flooded his mind.

'Last night,' he burst out. Offering body to the sun, he spoke to that sacred star, 'Last night!'

Pet scuttled and whimpered in excitement; his Master was pleased; his Master was a more awesome Master than ever. What joy! What honour! Pet could smell water on the air too and romped after his Master, he didn't lag behind on his lead as Beast strode out.

A mile or so before they reached the oasis, for oasis it was,

Beast took a robe and head dress from within his robe and dressed Pet. He washed Pet's face tenderly with precious drops of water. Pet simpered lovingly as Beast groomed him.

Beast carefully cleaned Pet's eyelashes, smoothed his hair, raised a traveller's flagon of luscious red wine to his lips, rubbed ointment on to the sunburn and whip welts on his body.

With a simple hand sign he gestured Pet to his knees before Master Therion, The Beast. He traced the sign of the cross, the four directions, upon Pet's forehead. Then he traced the points of a nine pointed star on his own chest. He tilted Pet's chin and signalled him to open his mouth, then lifting his own robe, he directed a thin dribble of deep gold urine into Pet's mouth. This was an oft repeated ritual. The two men held eye contact, their faces alight with heroism and intelligence. They had come to the desert and accomplished their mission. Their respective magickal grades were raised.

Side by side they walked at ease, as if on a familiar seaside promenade, comrades refreshed in mutual company, free of oppressive thoughts and ideas, free of all pointless habits. They were inhabited only, as the oasis came into view, by tranquil joy, the reward for those who have repaid excitement with ecstasy, repaid ecstasy with travesty and repaid travesty with their soul, a soul whole, unpackaged and unpartitioned.

Their faces and hands were brown, their minds masculine and cunning and at one with their destiny. These men were as natives here - men of the desert, children of extremes.

7.2   Est Gets Possessive

'Stritch, you can't go back to her!' Est stood in the middle of her front room upon the diamond shaped central pattern of an Afghan rug. She was rigid and aggressive, lips twitching, eyes overeager. Although their meetings came but once a month, with the full moon, they were intensely interested in one another.

Stritch shrugged and traced the carpet design with his heel. They were intimately close; a hair's breath divided them.

'If you go back to that filthy, disgusting old hag...' Est spluttered, incensed. 'I'll...'

'Shag.' His mouth was dry but he kept his cool.

'Do you shag her now too?'

'That's her name. Mama Shag.' Stritch's hollow eyes were Goth sexy boy careless intense. He moved imperceptibly nearer Est; their lips drew close as if by magick.

Est resisted the pleasure of his lips, although she loved his desire for her more than anything.

'I am too like you.' Speech meant she could avoid their lips meeting in a kiss.

'You are me.' He drew closer still, as if squeezing air out of the space between them. 'Most of me died,' he continued, 'when I left my family, my friends. Now all the parts of me that died have become you.'

'Narcissism! Is that why you find me fascinating?'

'You know that isn't it.' Negative forces blew towards him, then reacted to Est's energy and blew away.

'Temptation?' she asked.

'No, not that. The last temptation is innocence.' This was an important concept for him.

'What has that got to do with anything?'

'Nothing to do with anything. It is art.'

'Look; it's the middle of the night. Are you really going?' She moved away from the abstract.

'I have to,' Stritch responded simply.

'I'll make coffee for you.' Their hands joined in a moment of trust.

'No need; I must go.'

'Are you walking?'

He nodded. Est was forlorn and wouldn't watch as he left her apartment. She was glad he was leaving, really. She'd resisted him, so of course he'd go. Go somewhere he wouldn't be resisted, nor have to face deep emotions.

She was not going to fall into his arms, wouldn't lose herself in a black hole and never return.

Stritch said he'd seen god and that's why he was like he was, most of him dead and the dead parts *her*. How could she be his dead self? Though curiously it rang true to her. She did feel herself to be the part of Stritch he could no longer find, had lost hold of in a long nightmare. The trauma of nightmare went on and on until there was no pathway back, he could only remember himself through Est. 'And not then all the time,' she remarked to herself in angry understanding. 'Stritch only remembers himself through me when I yearn for The Magician. It's not me he wants; it's the results of my passion for that magickal creature of completion, the one whose life formula is aligned with the excessive energy released at the moment of creation.'

Stritch hunted for moments of extreme energy, Est for the source of these moments. And The Magician? The Beast, our hero Drummond, for what did he search? The next high? Supreme occult scholarship? The best shag ever? The meaning of the best shag ever, when, as in a fairy story, she came to him under cover of darkness?

It was as a fairy story the night Stritch had run away from his family home. He'd run through woods in a state of total poetry, with all the eagerness of antiadventure. Until, in a clearing in the wood he'd come upon an old woman dancing naked around a fire.

Her arms had gracefully traced the rhythmic patterns of the flames. Stritch had recalled his senses somewhat as she'd danced towards him, her flesh mottled and veined. She, eccentric and self-possessed, she, Mama Shag.

7.3   Starting With A Kiss

'My dear boy.' Beast patted Pet's hand, emotion intensified between them as the sandstorm blew ferociously outside their tent. Beast addressed Pet as 'boy' despite their parity in years. Beast leant forward from his cross legged position and kissed Pet softly, ritually, methodically once upon each eyelid and once fulsomely upon the lips. A rare kiss given for pleasure alone.

Beast drew deeply upon a brass hookah. 'There is nothing like a good smoke when the world is howling about one's ears.' The water in the hookah bubbled. Pet joined his Master in relaxation and intoxication.

Swathes of carpets covered the ground, flat weaves with patterns describing the herding of camels and goats, pile carpets tightly knotted, made on mobile looms carried by nomads taking their herd to pastures new; patterns of irrigated gardens in semi-settled territories, telling the wild excitement of small walled towns, of gambling and fighting. Upon these carpets Beast was comfortable. A man of expanded intellect and little deep feeling, he was at home in general conversation in more than twenty languages.

He had a fine ear for what one human being wished to comm-unicate to another. Strange, for a magician, that he was so wholly unaware of that other language, the language of silence. The skills of silence were a casualty to Beast's inherent egoism. 'You are the very devil,' his mother had said to him, 'the Antichrist of whom we have all been warned and it is my fate to be mother to such fiend.'

Pet made thickly sweet mint tea on a small kerosene stove. They sipped the sickly stuff from glasses with dainty handles. Beast began to answer a question Pet had asked him about the necessity of animal sacrifice. 'You see, my dear boy,' a brief moment of direct eye contact, 'the laws of magick are the laws of nature. Brutal and ferocious they may be, but they are the laws of inherent power. And power is what a man needs if he is to become more than a man, initiate and knowing.

'As a man I must exercise my Will at all times, for my Will is what keeps me from the brutishness of seeking sensation simply for sensation's sake, a place where addictive need for experiential violence quickly develops and sacrifice becomes ever more loathsome and perverse. No, this cannot be our way; sacrifice is a symbolic act.'

'If it is symbolic, why then the need for actual blood spilling?' queried Pet.

'Because a human being is created through the laws of nature and is therefore beholden unto them. He lives under the infantile rules of "cause and effect" and "seeing is believing". He cannot believe that each living being contains a unique energy that he, as a wilful being, can tap into and harness as his own, unless he ex- periences this energy as it is released at the point death.'

'Are we then to aspire to *human* sacrifice?' Pet raised his bushy eyebrows.

Beast tossed his head back 'Ha!' His laughter rang out like a sporting shot fired into the air, missing its fowl target. 'You would goad me beyond the honourable terrain of a gentleman?'

'You would utterly rule out human sacrifice?' persisted Pet.

'I would rule out overt cruelty, for he who practices cruelty is sure to have cruelty practiced upon him, as any man of the desert will tell you, if you can stand his undisciplined company long enough to hear his wise words.'

'Why then are the men of the desert ruthless towards one another?' asked Pet.

The conversation followed the lateral intellectual pattern of hashish.

'If you closely observe their habits and customs you will find that their ruthless actions are never done as one man to another, but as one representative of one tribe to the representative of another.

'Ruthlessness is never practiced from egotistical source in the desert. Thus the pride and dignity of the people we live amongst. Every person is unique where there is no bland uniform expression of rampant nature to countermand that claim to uniqueness. This is why the desert is the perfect place for magickal practice.' Beast closed his heavy eyelids. His hookah on one side of him, his empty glass the other, a hand outstretched upon each knee. Thumb and index finger joined, his chin dropped on to his collar bone. He inhaled deeply and tightened the muscles along his spine. He exhaled fully and again inhaled. After some time of deep breathing, he became attuned to the swirls and gusts of the storm outside.

Wind rippled the stout tent cloth. Pet listened attentively for the message within sound, listened for the manifestation of Beast's Will. Sure enough the wind calmed; Pet was proud of his Master's control of the wind.

As the wind died down, human noises outside penetrated the tent, staccato shouts of people calling to one another, until one loud shout arrived at their tent flap.

A Cheshire cat grin spread across Beast's face.

'I think we have visitors,' he said, in voice as fresh as iced lime. 'Do invite them in my dear boy.'

7.4   A Tarot Reading

Est cast off her shawl and listened to Claudia breathe through the thin partition wall that separated her bedroom from their living quarters.

She rattled the few pieces of coal that still smouldered in the grate; their orange glow was the only light in the room. She needed more to read cards by. She lit a candle from the fire. A drop of wax melted and dripped into the coals; a small yellow and blue flame rose up to consume it. She took a pinch of sandalwood powder from her pocket and sprinkled it in the fire.

Incense enwrapped her. She reached into her tatty sideboard for the blue Thai silk that covered her tarot cards. She spread the silk out in front of her, it flowed across the rug like the river of life. She focused her mind on the dilemma she wished to unravel and took the cards from their box. 'How can I know more of Stritch, my lover, and how does he relate to my search for The Magician?'

In the place where Stritch had stood the mist of his astral appeared; he had not altogether left her. The mist swirled slightly as Est shuffled the large cards dextrously; their smooth sides slid against one another.

Her concentration wavered; she was tempted towards the banal state of mind of 'he loves me, he loves me not,' but Est had not travelled such distance outside the comfort of convention to be lured by the low romance of sentiment.

She laid down seven cards in the upper arc of her unique 'fisheye' formation and the five of its lower edge.

The upper arc represented current circumstances, the lower the past and future commingling in Destiny's web.

Three central cards concerned Claudia and one final card in the corner of the eye was herself. She turned this card over first; it was the knight of swords indicating that she was tracked by the one she sought and suggested the question, 'When both are immersed in illusion, how can recognition occur?'

She turned next to the three central cards which concerned Claudia's growth.

The cards were: nine of cups, queen of swords and king of hearts. Claudia's happiness depended on an alchemical reaction within Est between 'woman of mystery' and 'king of plenty'.

Est relaxed; whatever way the remaining cards blew, her ability to protect Claudia was assured, so she could stomach all.

She interpreted the upper curve of cards:

'The purpose is with great dignity and enterprise to amass material enough to construct a well built home on firm foundations. It is not possible to do this unless the correct sacrifices have been made. In spite of endeavour, harmony, love and courage, if evil is the final invocation then evil will prevail. If the wind blows from the east do not embark on a project which requires the wind to blow from the west. Do not step yet beyond the realms of preparation; the time is not yet right for a journey. The teeth of vitality sucking demons (vampirish and insincere) may be withdrawn and the demons may smile with temporary ease. Do not be taken in. Make yourself vulnerable for one moment and you will be pounced upon. The present is a matter of great restraint.'

She looked at the arrangement of the five cards of the lower arc, to interpret the time and direction of her journey in relation to Claudia, Stritch and Master Therion, The Magician.

'It is lonely and cold to stand upon high arid ground but it is only from this position that enough of the world can be seen to anticipate the attacks of one's enemies. There are many enemies as you approach the fulfilment of your innocence and your original needs and your soul shudders. Remain humble in dress and attitude and noble patronage will help you on your way. Do not look beyond the ordinary and common. Do well what is available for all to work upon. Small steps are advantageous.'

Est completed her reading by re-ordering the cards. It was as she thought, she was still living under the auspices of evil, a position she had vowed to work her way away from. The dark side had once entirely swamped her life. She must continue to work with the part of herself she had managed to salvage from demonic influence and accept the restraints and limitations this placed upon her. She had to stay where she could see clearly, she could not venture into the twilight regions of illusion.

7.5   On The Move

'And now my dear boy,' Beast patted Pet's hand in familiar gesture, 'we are bound for Europe, where, with raw energy and cheering new magickal grades, we will found an Abbey'. Beast smiled beatifically, with eyes of such luminosity as proved to Pet that Beast was Magus no longer, was Ipsissimus (extreme self) with all the universe incorporated in realisable consciousness.

'The men, women and children of this Oasis depend upon you; you cannot leave,' replied Pet, even while anxiously noticing that he had an erection brought on by the idea of a new project.

'Depend on me! These wild glamorous romantic people? I think not. My dear Adeptus indispensablus, in spite of my elevated occult grade, I am still a man, albeit a man with the awareness of a god. Does that give me godly power?' Beast's laughter got the better of him and he rolled around the rugs covering their tent floor. 'Yes, I feel now,' (more laughter), 'that I do have the power of a god, though am not as well endowed as you, you mischievous satyr.'

Beast resumed a contemplative cross-legged position.

'I spent twenty years developing my ego and not for one moment did ego fail me. I revelled in life, gave myself to sensual pleasure, to drink, women, heightened perception. I embraced all stimulation to the utmost limits. Not once did extremity fail to amuse me, remarkable as this may seem. Put this down to good fortune, in character, background and companionship if you will, all of which, I affirm, were mine. But I regard this process of sensual exploration as magickal, an expression of the workings of my unique destiny.'

Drummond's destiny, the Beastly career!

'I was then fatefully guided to initiation. I grew in wisdom and knowledge as I had grown in the world. As my magickal grade rose I left off the habits of a man of style and fashion and took on those of the adept, then Magus and now Ipsissimus!'

Pet, true to his scholarly self, wrote in a notebook as he sat in full lotus position.

In mutual concentration, time was driven from the tent. Outside the sounds of nature panted and puffed as the desert people worked and called to one another amidst the aromatic assault of cardamom and myrrh. The stimulation of scent is catalyst to occult perception. The two men in unequivocal accord, sat until the sands of time ran backwards, without conversation and the assumptions that accompany it.

Barely with breath, for little air is needed when the body is quiet, Beast and Pet travelled out of the physical dimension. They stayed thus for as long as it took to *relax* and surface refreshed. Pet beamed idiotically and then remembered to be Adeptus serious. Beast showed the majesty of his position by the marks of anxiety upon his brow and around the deep downward curve of his dogfish mouth, full of teeth browned by tobacco and kif.

'The crucial grades of Adeptus, Magus and Ipsissimus' - he said the last word with ponderous gravity -, 'are equivalent in esoteric terms to the physical development of foetus, child and adult. The transition from Adept to Magus is traumatic and dangerous as is the process of birth. And like birth it requires the body of the woman, the Scarlet Woman devoted absolutely to the realisation of creation. Without a woman willing to lay down her life (if necessary) the grade of Magus cannot be attained. My first Scarlet Woman, my first wife Irene, bravely addressed her task. I thought her little more than an exceptionally bright and pretty face with a willingness to, shall we say, have a good time. We had a good time. I passed through Adeptus Minor, Adeptus Major and as I approached Adeptus Exempt her vision reached a clarity I had not imagined possible from a woman in whalebone. She became more than I'd dreamt she could ever be. How wrong can an Adept be! Sorry Pet; I repeat myself. I must get to the point; the prospect of travel is perhaps a little wearying.

'She gave me the vision of the Law, The Law of Thelema. The crisis, the peak and the glory of the Law. Love is the Law, Love under Will.

'It was worth her sanity to contribute in such passionate way to the history of philosophy, the history of mankind, to the construction of future culture.'

In accord, the two men sorted through the possessions they had accumulated at the Oasis, in preparation for their departure.

Chapter 8

8.1 Can This Love Be Reciprocal?

'You have found me.' Lillian was slouched against the summer house's wooden frame.

'I have looked everywhere.' Mahoney puffed up two steps as if climbing Canary Wharf.

The summer house was octagonal and open on all sides, although it nestled in a shady glen in *Rideland*'s grounds. Lillian wore a short sleeved frock in lightweight black cotton with an innocuous floral print. She was relaxed in spite of arms gone to goose pimples. Her wide mouth and fat lips attracted Mahoney anew. Light faded three shades as he stumbled across creaking boards to her; he shivered in his vest and light summer shirt. His trousers slid down his bottom.

He wanted to hold her close and kiss her; he didn't want to face the lost and lonely feeling inside his stomach, beneath limp underwear and undergroomed flesh. He wanted to stop up his emotional black hole with the freedom she carried within her, and release himself into perfectly ordered stanzas celebrating his woman.

Lillian spoke as if she'd been reading his thoughts. 'I am not your Muse, am not she who can release your genius.' She kissed his freckled nose.

'But?'

'I know you mean well. You are a kind poet and a good person, but morality and talent mean nothing to me, count for nothing in the magickal world you have entered.'

Words drifted as shadows melted into twilight mauve. A drop of rain fell on Mahoney's neck.

'What are you if not my muse?'

She shook her head in soft negative.

'What are you to become if not my muse?' Mahoney persisted.

'An intelligent question! You are a woodlouse learning to weave a web.'

'I have been caught in a web; I do not weave.' He pouted petulantly.

She blew him a kiss. 'No more similes. Let us refresh ourselves; look what I have brought! With all this waiting consider yourself lucky I haven't polished it off. Here, whisky, scones, hard boiled eggs, lettuce and apples.' Lillian twirled an apple on its stalk. She offered it to Mahoney with a beaker of amber nectar. He took both greedily.

'I am ravenous. Thank you so much; you think of everything.'

'Let's feast.' She drank whisky in fishy gulps.

'I thought I saw you in a thousand places. Thought you called my name.' Mahoney spoke words of love. 'Frustrated, I rolled in daisies and plantain hoping you would see me. I called your name to sky and house. Trees answered; they spoke of you.'

Lillian used a sharp pocket knife to slice hard boiled egg neatly into a scone. She added a lettuce heart and handed the assemblage to Mahoney.

'Supernatural voices.' Lillian nibbled an egg and gazed at him. 'You have seen the boundary of the grounds?'

Mahoney washed scone down with whisky. She handed him more of both.

'You know I've never enjoyed food so much. It is as if I never tasted egg, apple or scone before. Even the butter has a distinctive flavour. Usually I don't care what I eat and barely taste the food. I must be in love! Lillian I am in love with you!' Overjoyed.

'You cannot evade my question as easily as that.'

'How can a declaration of love be evasion?'

'Easily. You know nothing. Get up off your knee,' she ordered, quietly sinister. Exit sun: pinks and lilacs diffused finally to greyscale.

'I want to marry you Lillian. Be my wife, you have made a new man of me. Before meeting you I was a creature without limbs or purpose, limits or pleasures.'

'Mahoney, I could be icy cold or grateful; any reaction to this would be self indulgence. Remember we are not here to stuff up the plugholes inside us that say "this way to the abyss," nor to initiate an escapist coupling to maintain our lives in holy stagnancy. We are here to commit crimes against monogamy, against convention; crimes against Christianity. It is exciting and unnerving.' She raised her replenished beaker and he followed suit, eager to butter her up and shag her again, which he wanted to do above anything.

'I will do anything to stay with you.'

'Obedience is of some use.' Lillian drew one of Mahoney's hands up her frock. 'But remember, being already whore, wife and mistress, I have no vacant role. Accept that as The Beast's Scarlet Woman I am sexually experimental. Enjoy your occult role.'

'My dearest Lillian,'

'Animal, please.'

'My dearest Animal, I am forever in your debt.'

Summer rain pattered down, then quickened to urgent rhythm. A few drops dripped through the roof on to Lillian's lap. She did not react or move away.

Mahoney was in a surreal state of waiting, akin to love. He had difficulty keeping his mind clear. Meanwhile bird life in willow and ash usurped his senses, enticing them from monogamous mind monotony, probably the prime function of bird song for the human. A cooing wood pigeon evoked deep nostalgia, it being the first bird call he had learned to identify as a boy. Its guttural psalm echoed through the steam of summer evening rain.

'The world is dark and empty when one is all ears,' thought Mahoney as Lillian opened her huge mouth.

'This is the place,' Lillian's words were flying ants spinning in infinite quantity round Mahoney's head, 'where my Beast came with the Lady of the House after he'd been driven from Cambridge by the demons of convention and Christianity. It was here they discovered magick beyond the dynamic of black and white. It was here that polarity dissolved in the radiance of their combined Will. Can you feel the vital spirit of Love?'

'For me love is personal, intimate, unique, entirely compatible with Christianity.'

'And monogamy?' she asked as playfully as a leopard.

'Of course monogamy. That is a prerequisite for love?' He reached for her hand, but she had surreptitiously slid along the bench.

'Love is inherently monogamous?' Her mesmeric words penetrated him. Rain eased. Darkness was a thick black bandage over his eyes. She laughed.

He had always thought life a haphazard warm affair; this woman creature would have it quite otherwise. She was no chaotic specimen, no member of no ant warren, she was a fabulous creature camouflaged within night, challenging his infinite cowardice. Newly evolved space within him teemed with life. He had passed through the land of déjà vu to enter the world of the elect, initiate. A growl rumbled in his throat.

A bell from the house peeled four times.

'Come.' Lillian's eyes were red with unspeakable passion. 'It is time to show you how Beast lost his earthly parents, Time and Disease.' She smoothed her bedraggled dress. In humid night air Mahoney smelt earthworms, leaf mould and Lillian/Animal's hot female stench.

She bent down and pulled at a metal ring in the floorboards that Mahoney had not noticed before. A trap door opened, children's adventure story style. He and Animal grinned fat cat grins at one another. He gestured chivalrously for her to descend first, where six steps led underground. A faint light glowed at the bottom of the steps. 'A rush taper perhaps,' thought Mahoney, enjoying himself in a way he had not done for a minimum of 20 years.

'More like a hex a minute,' Animal answered his thoughts.

Six steps hacked in earth reinforced with rotting pieces of wood which broke as they descended. They came to a small passageway, riskily in need of extra roof support. A stone rattled behind them as they passed. Another six steps took them down into a cavern where riveted steel supported the roof, a place worth waiting, bored, half your life to see.

The cavern was lit by many candles in metal holders bolted to the wall. In the circular room the curved steel supports gave the sensation of being inside a tortoise's belly.

A black curtain fell into place behind them. Upon the curtain was embroidered a gold pentacle; two circles enclosed it and a third circle was drawn in the centre of the pentacle. The language of symbols lent the room glamour. The floor was laid in a mosaic of labyrinthine pattern, brain dizzyingly complex.

There was an altar opposite where Animal and Mahoney stood. It was studded with pieces of mirror, reflecting candlelight. A bright shaft of this reflected light painfully pierced Mahoney's eye. A robed and hooded figure behind the altar raised her arms and called, 'Come,' a tempting syllable. Dramatically she held a wand in one hand, a sword in the other. 'It is time. Welcome, Hounds of Hell and Cats of the Wilderness!'

8.2   Underground Ritual

A lightning bolt engendered within Mama Shag, The Lady of the House, manifested blue-white from the end of her sword, held in her right hand. At the tip of her wand held in her left hand, a swirling vacuum appeared. She touched wand to sword, to balance their respective powers. The black hood fell from her weather worn face. She was powerfully mature, animated with vitality gleaned from a fully experimental life.

She smiled a salacious Bishop's smile and placed sword and wand upon the altar in what, by contrast to her recent pyrotechnics, was a domestic gesture.

Her robe scintillated as candlelight picked out its golden threads, woven through black.

She addressed Mahoney.

'You wish to become free of the ordinary fetters of humanity?' Mahoney opened and closed his mouth, fish style. The Lady of the House nodded decisively.

'You need a name. Animal, dress our initiate and we will proceed.'

Animal took a red robe from a brass peg by the entrance and helped him into it, covering his head with its hood. She dressed herself likewise.

The cavern breathed soft silence. Mahoney was comfortable in the robe which smoothed the unaesthetic contours of his body. His soul expanded; he felt ready for anything.

The Lady of the House took a small silver bell from the altar where it rested beside a large trophy. At its high pitched 'ting' a figure emerged from the wall. He had been standing very still against the curved plaster and Mahoney had not noticed him.

This white robed figure placed his hands together and bowed briefly to the Lady of the House; she bowed back. He then took his place to her left behind the altar, with Animal on her right. Mahoney floundered, alone, in the open arena of the cavern. Space spun around him; he raised his eyes in an appeal for divine guidance before his knees gave way.

'Come.' The Lady of the House's voice was awesome, without trace of the kitchen duenna she had so recently been. She beckoned Mahoney. 'Rise and come hither.'

She instructed her two assistants, 'Prepare the cup and horn.'

Poor Mahoney could not rise; his feet slipped upon the labyrinthine patterned floor. His body felt like uncontained oil oozing through the mosaic into earth. He choked, fought for believable definition of self.

'Come,' commanded the Lady of the House, raising the pitch of her voice. A titter came from the two assistants who had themselves been in Mahoney's place.

The only way Mahoney could 'come' was to crawl. His knees slid upon the tiles, gave way and he sprawled belly down; his ceremonial robe rode up to his waist; underneath were his dirty trousers. A fag butt rolled out of a trouser turn up. He reached the altar after an interminable journey and grasped at the black altar cloth. The altar itself was raised on a podium where the other three ritual participants stood.

'I think not,' Our Lady's voice rang out, as Mahoney made to pull himself up by tugging the altar cloth. 'Stand.'

The power of her voice pulled him to his feet; his head flopped on a weak neck but the rest of his body stood straight enough. His tongue lolled out of the side of his mouth.

'Drink from my cup.' Our Lady held a pewter cup above her head; then she brought it to her lips and took a sip of wine, smacking her lips with animal enthusiasm. She held the cup out to Mahoney across the altar. The taste of wine revived him. 'Mmm!' He drained the cup.

'Are you ready?' Our Lady's eyes glinted with humour; her two assistants giggled conspiratorially.

'I am ready for anything!' But Mahoney's words fell flat.

Our Lady, Mama Shag, nodded and the two assistants came from behind the altar to stand one each side of him. The white robed figure carried a small piece of highly polished silver on which was a mound of white powder; he carried this offering carefully so as not to disturb the powder; he mustn't let it blow away. Animal, in red, carried a silver pipe.

'No.' Mahoney might be an alcoholic but he did not touch drugs. 'Powders, no thank you.' The assistants moved in; Animal grasped his arms behind his back. Mahoney was immobilised as the white robed stranger tipped the pyramid of crystalline powder into his undisciplined jaws.

Our Lady crossed her arms hand to shoulder, hand to shoulder, ringing the bell twice. Animal slipped a black hood over Mahoney's head as cocaine exploded in adorable, destructive fragments throughout his mind.

Darkness glowed rich as the assistants' breath raised the tiny hairs on Mahoney's skin. Light feet pattered around the chamber evidently extinguishing candles, for when his hood was removed the invasive push of utter darkness flooded his senses. He felt warm breath on his face as humans approached, humans he could detect only by their blood heat and the displacement of air around him. Three disrobed humans touched him. He blushed hard at the touch of unmistakeably male flesh.

He was rigid with tension as a sword ripped the clothes from his body. No fiddling with buttons for this demonic hoard. His underpants stuck around the crotch where he'd been sweating heavily since his ladylove had led him into this ritual ordeal. He remained stock still, his left eye twitching as clothing fell from him. He wished his garments would show some decent reluctance or his character some courageous defiance. Neither. Blood pounded in his head; he felt he had an invisible nose bleed as his sexual rod stood to attention.

'No,' he groaned and fell to his knees again. Bare arms plus breasts cradled him from behind and a mouth enclosed his lingam.

'No.' If the breasts were behind him, sure as sure the lingam was in front. The soft persuasive mouth eliciting shudders and gasps had to be part of the same body as a phallic rod.

His perception that Animal was behind him and the thin white robed stranger was giving him head received a serious new angle as the head of a penis nudged his anal sphincter. Like an ambitious woman's mind the velvety head eased its way inbetween his hairy arse cheeks, insistently pushing in. He cried out, though it wasn't his first time was it? Beast had done it, hadn't he? And it wasn't really pain, was it?

Super-arousal is a kind of exhaustion, but Mahoney wouldn't

107

come yet, not with those long licks on the underside of his lingam, tongue tip working its way into the groove in the head and up to the hole of emission. There was no emission, for cocaine was holding him back. His spine contorted, hips thrust beyond his control or usual frame of reference. One lady that was his thing; Love, that was his thing.

What was this? Precise business-like bodies gave him the cold shivers with their icy professionalism. But it didn't turn him off. He was desperate for emission to cool the volcanic heat of his body and then to escape.

'Let me out of here!' he cried at the top of his voice which however, didn't come out very loud, was more of an unconvincing croak.

And he wasn't disappointed when a belt as cold as frozen iron snapped into position around his waist and chains clipped on the iron as bracelets were fixed around his wrists and ankles. And exquisite loveliness! A rigid collar was placed around his neck! The metal was unendurably heavy unless he kept his head in exactly the right position. He was on his knees, manacled and happy.

'God,' he pleaded as the last chain was clipped into place and alarm was replaced by all-embracing resignation; he trusted these people. He was in love with wondrous Lillian who had brought him here to release him from the trivia that had enslaved his soul. Waves of gratitude swept through him. But again he clung to a final conclusion of monogamous coupling. He longed to be alone with his Lillian on the big bed, her lovely clitoris laid open for his eyes, for all his greediness.

But he was not going to be allowed to stay contented, for here came rough old fingers greasing his anus with white jelly as if he was a dead chicken.

This time the lingam didn't wait; it slid into his arse and went true and deep, as they say, right up to the hilt. The penetrating lingam ripped apart the division between pain and pleasure, heaven and hell and the fetid heat around him burst into purple stars. A mouth teased his testicles; a face rough with stubble brushed his thigh. A man? Two men? How come two men? With biting teeth upon his nipples his chest swelled. The mouth that licked and bit belonged to the same face that had a smooth female hair-free cheek, but not young and plump. Our Lady's mouth was on his nipples he supposed. Her attention to his nipples turned his chest to breasts; his body shuddered but he could not move; the heavy manacles clanked together and cut into him.

He groaned as all pleasure subsided due to hard anal thrusting; it was endurance for him now. And in this bleakness he no longer cared where he was, could only feel the eternity that was inescapable pain. His lingam shot off semen in mid air as his head exploded. His sweat worked with the friction of metal on skin to create blisters and blood.

Exhausted he fell heavily into the manacles, unable to support his own weight.

The bodies moved away. His head rolled to one side in a long anaesthetising pause, a separation of mind and body. He didn't feel like a limbed mammal, but a vast carnivorous entity, stranded away from ordinary form yet not sufficiently initiate to inhabit the true form of his ethereal self.

A maternal voice clung in his mind sucking on childhood memories.

'Who are you?' asked Our Lady. Silence followed, a perceptive quietude that seemed to beckon alien creatures in amazing space-craft.

'Who are you?' Soft and persuasive, the sort of voice you could share a meal with. It triggered thoughts of animal pleasures and sent spasms of stomach wrenching pain to grip Mahoney in a vice that romped around the pain scale to settle to a throbbing and partially numbing series of cramps. The clenching spasms of pain became less bearable as silence pulsed all around him.

He was far from the streams and glades of home where pine trees dripped resinous rain on to his forehead and rain trickled in rivulets over the backs of his hands. Home. He heard his voice, eventually answering the 'whoareyou?' question.

'I am a hound. I am a Hound of Hell!'

A choral unison of voices responded in a chant with religious purpose unknown to any prior or abbess outside de Sade.

'Welcome. Thrice welcome Hound of Hell, you will serve us. Discover yourself. Love is the law, Love under will. Welcome.'

In one clash his manacles were released and he fell prone in a clichéd posture of surrender.

Warm bodies came and lay on the floor beside him, covered him with attentive licks and kisses, stroked him, fondled him. They grunted and purred until an easy repose settled them and they rested awhile, as they were, upon the cold cavern floor, naked bodies warming each other.

'Hound.' Lillian's voice. 'Hound.' Mahoney woke, his body trapped between others.

'Hound look at me.'

She sat on a step a candle by her crotch, her knees up, legs spread. There between her legs, where he'd been with his fingers, his tongue, his lingam, there between pink labia a penis rose erect. Animal laughed gleefully and put one finger into her vaginal hole at the base of her lingam! She took out her finger, licked it lightly then used it to show another hole, her anus. She beckoned him.

He slithered out from between bodies.

'Come in me. Come inside me.' She stroked her impressive red penis. 'Hound come in me.'

'I'm not?'

'Yes you are. You're one of us now.' She playfully tugged a curly lock and tucked it behind his ear. 'You're Hound and I'm Animal. We'll have a good time. You always wanted to be one of us, didn't you?' She opened her legs wider and parted her labia with two fingers to show pearly drops bubbling in her vagina. She knew how to tempt him, penis or no penis.

'Don't be shy,' she teased. 'We all know how much you like

penises. You like to feel them inside you don't you? So do I. Come on. Please me as you can.'

She was irresistible; he pushed her gently back and his own lingam plunged deep in her very womanly vagina, her manhood rubbing his belly; she dripped pre-come onto him. No definition of pleasure he had as yet learned was equal to this experience. A lithe figure crept up behind him and pain exploded in his anus. He was buggered again. Buggered while mounting a woman with a penis. All he needed was a goat to menstruate on his face for his evening to be complete.

Chapter 9

9.1 Est's Family Life

Est had caught the dangerous musk of male in dreams, these nights since Stritch had last visited. Dreams without pictures, dreams to which she was olfactory witness.

Her dead senses stirred awakening dormant functions. Ears flapped, nose wriggled, toes were as clever as fingers. With the scent of musk she imagined herself tailed. Passionate monkey fear swept through her 5 a.m. lucid dream. Trying to wake she entered a black tunnel at roller coaster speed. Excitement peaked as an orange pinpoint of light at the end of the ride burst into stellar lilac. The ride chugged to a standstill but it was not over; she was plunged into a new experience. She slid off the roller coaster rails to float, surrounded by an array of white particles gleaming phosphorescently within universal black. These particles gelled to form bones which spun together and created a skeleton which danced towards her. Fear, as bones crashed through her eyes! Dizzily she fell, while white bones glowed in a black vortex and she was pulled upwards through a compressed universe. The bones deteriorated into original energy and in profound stillness she witnessed the majesty of galaxy 86.

Happily, she recalled she'd been here before. Pleasure however, was short lived; she had to appear before her maker (designer of skeletons, decoder of dreams) to be judged. She attempted a defence but unfamiliar words tumbled heavy and material from her lips, impregnated with desire transcending societal expectation. 'Shugal Choronzon, Shugal Choronzon, Shugal Choronzon.'

She could not quite pull her body from sleep. Anyway, why should she resist these delicious scents awakening her latent parts? Heady, they came in waves of exotic sandalwood and musk.

Then a large spider crawled up her leg and she sat up in bed suddenly. 'What was that?' She moved to brush off the spider. She was naked, the covers thrown off except for a strip of coarse wool blanket over her left leg. It must have been the blanket she'd felt, she decided, rubbing her eyes. These rich dreams made her sick; she rushed to the bathroom clutching her stomach.

Her child cried out for her.

'Just coming darling. It's alright; I won't be a moment,' Est called.

Claudia sleepily came into the bathroom where Est was washing her hands after being sick.

'Are you alright darling?'

'I'm scared.'

'Have a glass of water. Here, I'll get it for you. Drink this. Did you have a bad dream?'

'The monsters came to get me.'

'Were they horrible monsters?'

'They were great big blue monsters and they'd eaten all my toys and...' Claudia cuddled her mother, burying her tousled head into comforting mother belly.

'Come on now.' Arms round one another they drifted back into Est's dawn speckled bed.

'I don't feel well; I have a tummy ache,' pleaded Claudia.

'Does it hurt very much?'

Claudia nodded. 'Can I stay at home with you today?'

'Alright. You seem to stay at home with me every day. Don't you like going to school with the other girls?'

'Well...'

'What is it you don't like about it?'

'Well...'

'I'll make a cup of tea. Come on, move over so I can get my legs out of this bed.'

'The other girls say I haven't got a father. I have got a father, haven't I?'

'Of course you've got a father; everybody has a father.' Est

113

filled the kettle.

The water boiled. Est poured a dash into a teapot and two cups to warm them. The tiny basement kitchen was dark even in waxing morning light. Solitary sunrays lit up patches of the stone floor. An earwig rushed across a sunray spotlight.

Est poured boiling water on to tealeaves, cut slices of brown bread and spread them with margarine. Claudia made a face; the tea was hot and bitter.

'Do you want to help me mix the purple paint again today?' Est asked.

'Can I paint a picture?'

'Yes of course you can. Here paint over this.'

'That's your lovely picture of the sky.'

'It doesn't matter; no one wants my pictures anyway.'

'Isn't a man going to come and buy some again?'

'I don't think so.'

Est and Claudia were bored with bread and tea, all there was between themselves and hunger. Bread, tea and Maltby. 'Are you my father?' Claudia had asked Maltby. He wasn't though.

A note came asking for school fees. No, Est replied, Claudia would not be returning to school. Yes, she would pay the outstanding fees when she could and was sorry, for Claudia's sake, if she had breached a commitment. But unfortunately, unforeseen circumstances and so on...

*   *   *

Later that week Est and Claudia were on one of their wanders around the provincial city streets, when Claudia found an old sack in a back street. It was stuffed full of men's clothes and a pair of shoes, all in good condition. With a little alteration they fitted Est well.

'Look at me Claudia! How do I look?'

'Like a man Est,' Claudia stated, matter of fact.

'I know, a *man*.' Est was excited and a little impatient with her daughter. 'I mean what kind of man. A smart gentlemanlike man, a rich man, a dashing man about town?' She tipped the brim of her hat to a racy angle.

'Like tinker, tailor, soldier, sailor, richman, poorman, beggarman, spy.'

'Beggarman, thief,' corrected her mother.

'Spy for me. I don't like any of the others.' Claudia curled her body in its grey-white nightdress closer to the half hearted fire. 'Why can't we have a proper hot fire?'

'If we used all the wood today, there'd be none left for the rest of the week.'

'Couldn't we burn coal?'

'Here. Put this jumper on.'

'It's itchy.'

Est shrugged. 'Maybe our luck will change with this suit. Why spy? Why not for instance, painter?'

'Oh Est, *not* a *painter*.'

'Why not?'

'Painters aren't real people; they don't even look happy when they smile.' Claudia jumped up and down lightly kicking her heels to her bottom. 'Tinker,' she said with one jump, 'tailor' with the next, 'soldier'. She reached 'spy' for the fifth time as a knock on the door interrupted her.

'Hello!' Maltby called.

'Darling Est,' he curled his elegant arm around her waist. 'You look fabulous.' He kissed her gently on the lips.

'Do I look like a man?'

'*You*, like a man? I think not.' She with her large bosom, undulating buttocks and long tapering fingers.

'Don't say that,' Est pouted. 'Maltby, I need to be a man.'

'It is marvellous,' thought Maltby, 'how she never bears the marks of poverty - boils and obsequiousness. Her paintbrush does away with it all. A genius certainly. Yes, she will do better as a man.'

He reached into his pocket; Claudia's eyes lit up expectantly. He handed her a sticky red lollipop, a little worse for wear with lint from his pocket.

He observed Est's besuited figure. 'Put the jacket on,' he instructed, thinking to cover her sensuous buttocks. 'Plus jacket you do look manly. Turn around. You must bandage up your bosom my dear. Minus bosom. Even a strong man would not have so much to declare, pectorally.'

'Stay there.' Est excitedly scampered into Claudia's box room, returning topless to the kitchen to rummage for binding material.

'You'll have to help me Maltby. I've got some rags but I can't get them round me.'

Claudia perched upon a kitchen chair sucking on her red lolly while Maltby bandaged Est's breasts.

'You're going to look round all over,' laughed Claudia. She slid from her perch and picked out a piece of warm charcoal from the fireplace. She stood on a chair and drew a neat moustache and dark eyebrows on her mother's face. 'She's a man, she's a man,' she chanted, 'a man and a spy.'

'Who Est dearest, are you going to spy on?' asked Maltby with interest.

'Spy? Perhaps,' Est replied, 'if a woman in disguise is a spy. However the disguise will not be complete until they who I wish to believe in it, are indeed duped.'

'I believe in their belief,' assured Maltby warming to Est's latest life experiment. He saw its necessity, for as a woman without friends or connections, she had small chance of selling her work. A woman could not be a free spirit and know success. A man on the other hand, would be judged by his work, not by his gender or character. On an assessment based on actual excellence Maltby was confident Est would shine.

Est's white shirt was buttoned, her tie and jacket in place.

'On looks you pass. Now learn to walk and talk like a man, to stand close to people and look them in the eye.'

Est leant against the wood wormy kitchen table. 'I shall smoke a pipe and drink claret, for fun. For real, I will sell paintings. These.' The wall was stacked with canvases.

Maltby tilted his head. 'The style's quite different, unrecognisable.'

'Do you like them?'

'She's painting like man, she *is* a man.' Claudia pranced around the limited space. 'Est's a man and I'm a boy. Do I make a good boy?' Claudia pulled a serious face, blew her cheeks out and walked with her chest pigeoned. 'How am I?'

'You're a fine boy for a ballet dancer, dear Claudia,' answered Maltby distractedly, concentrating on Est's paintings.

'Then that's what I'll be, a boy ballerina.' She leapt fawn like. 'No one's paying any attention to me.' She sneaked up behind Est and pulled her coat. 'How can you be a man with those great big boobies?'

'People judge more on what you appear to be than what you really are.'

'Why must you be a man anyway, Est?' She cuddled up to her mother.

'Good question Claudia. Well, if I am not to clean other people's houses I must sell paintings and it seems that art dealers do not want to buy paintings from a woman.'

'Why not?'

'They think women do not work consistently. Paintings only become sought after and consequently valuable if the painter continues working. Determination is not generally held to be a feminine quality.'

'But you'll go on painting?'

'I couldn't stop if I tried my darling.' She stroked Claudia's blonde locks back from her face. 'I will always paint. As a man I won't have to prove that; it will be taken for granted.'

'Will I have a career when I grow up? I'm going to be a ballerina, a boy ballerina. I'll spin like a lady and leap like a man.'

117

'A sublime combination. I shall come and see you dance every performance. Wild horses ridden by fearsome monster art dealers could not keep me away,' assured Maltby.

'Blue velvet curtains adorned with golden ropes will part. I appear through layers of rainbow gauze. I lift my swanlike arms and come to the front of the stage. The audience gasp for my hair is cut short like a man's and I wear trousers. I leap and spin. The applause drowns the sound of the big drums rolling out rhythm. I dance, summoning the other dancers from the wings; they wear brown tights and green tunics; they are trees come to life.'

'Pass me the scissors and I will cut my hair as short as the boy ballerina's.'

'Oh Est, don't, your lovely hair!' pleaded Claudia.

'I must pass as a man and earn our living.' Mother and daughter had quite forgotten about Maltby who was muttering at a painting:

'You have taken the colour out and added form where there was but light and movement. Your sense of proportion used to refer to negative space. Now you occupy the territory of action.'

'Quite male,' Est declared.

'Male? I wouldn't say male. Male enough to pass as male of course.' Mahoney the expert made his assessment of Est's paintings.

'Do you think they'll sell?'

'In London I don't know; in Paris, yes. Come on Est; Claudia, get dressed brush your hair. Let's have coffee and cake.'

'Cake! Can I have a chocolate éclair? The biggest one in the shop?' asked Claudia eagerly.

'You can have two,' allowed Maltby generously.

Est snipped her new short fringe even. 'Monsieur at your service. One large Scotch for me.'

'I shall join you in that my dear, shall we promenade?'

Chapter 10

10.1 More About Stritch

The Crystal Room was at the front of *Ridelands* on the first floor. This room had once been part of the long gallery, where ladies promenaded on wet days. Some of its former grandeur was still evident in the ceiling mouldings, where puce cherubs attended bare breasted Artemis. Floor length windows admitted hard northern light, above them a heavy black blind was folded to the ceiling. An altar stood before the windows, hewn from rock crystal. A sphere, a pyramid and a cube of obsidian sat upon its polished surface. The floor was an intricate mosaic of crystal pieces.

Lillian/Animal was late. Stritch had become impatient, unusual for him after the discipline of three years' self-imposed starvation.

'Where have you been Animal?' He put his arms around her and inhaled the particular scent of avocado that lurked behind her ears.

'Leave me alone Stritch, I'm not in the mood.' She moved to the window. The floor was stepped layers of crystal, a theatre in miniature.

'I've sacrificed everything to be with the Beast and to be here. But this Hound, this dumb Irish poet Mahoney is wearing me down.' She sat upon a step, leant against the window frame. 'Did you clean up in here? It's lovely; all the blood stains have gone.'

The pale young man nodded slightly. He wanted to get on. Animal was slowly reassured by the deep quiet of the room and Stritch's confidence. His presence sucked out the compassion that Mahoney's affection had planted in her.

'Don't you ever long for your life before?' Animal asked wistfully.

Stritch sat beside her, his knees bent to his chin. He took her hands and rubbed her thumbs. His body was a white bone stained here and there with nature's juices - grass, walnut, moss - tide lines of journeys he'd made. He smelt neutral in the same way a bog or a pond smelt neutral.

'I'm not alive in the way you are Animal. Compared to you I died a long time ago.' His voice was melodiously compelling.

'Yesterday I wasn't alive in the way I am today,' replied Animal. 'I was more like you. Today, I'm a mess.' She wrapped her fingers around his.

'It's his fear, not yours Animal. Don't let his fear draw you in.' Stritch glanced nonchalantly out of the window at the green scene and tapped on the glass with his nails to Mama Shag who was walking across the gravel to the monkey puzzle. Alert, she heard and gave him her broad ham smile.

'Is there something special between you two?'

'Animal of course there is; it's not personal though; is not more or less than any other specialness. It's not because I'm grateful she gave me a roof over my head when I was wandering and didn't know who I was.'

'No?'

'I would have left here by now if it had been that. There's no *reason* in the world I'd stay. It's simply my destiny.'

'I know what you mean. I feel the same.'

'Can we proceed?' He indicated the altar with a graceful movement.

'Not yet Stritch. How can I stop him from doing this to me?' Her wild eyes flickered over Stritch, perennially out of place in daylight.

Stritch ignored her question. 'Have you eaten?'

'Have you?'

'Me? Eaten?' They laughed.

'I haven't eaten for three days!' shouted Animal.

'I haven't eaten for, um, I can't remember.' Stritch smiled peacefully.

'You really can't remember when you took a bite from a sweet roll, warm from Mama Shag's oven and the aroma and flavour gave you intense pleasure?' Animal stretched. Stritch watched the thin dress slide over her breasts.

'Food could never do that for me,' he asserted.

'Nor me.' She made fists and drew them down the sides of her body.

'Today we shall eat together.' He pointed to a wicker hamper. 'We shall do together what you and that Hound have done and undo the affect he has had on you. Come dearest Animal, let us picnic.' They touched fingertips and imitating postures of medieval dancers, moved to the picnic hamper. Stritch threw back the lid with the tip of his toe, its toenail bruised purple.

Lillian recoiled as the hamper lid fell back against its leather hinges. She saw writhing snakes. Stritch did not and ignored her horror as he took a linen tablecloth from the basket and laid it out neatly upon the crystal platform before the altar.

Animal sat by the cloth with her legs folded beneath her. The crystal was cold. Each picnic item was a snake to her until Stritch's handling of the object informed otherwise. It required great concentration to lift a glass of wine to her lips and toast their hostess seeing all the while a small yellow snake in her hand. It was hard for her to believe it was not snake venom she swallowed down. It was even more difficult to chew upon snake's head which she assumed, in a parallel universe, was a roll.

'Another roll?' Stritch offered her a plate of seething brown and white snakes. 'With butter or without? Have some green salad from Mama's garden.'

Every mouthful was torture to Animal, while Stritch ate easily, from rolls and salad to chocolate cake.

'We have been fortunate with the weather all week?'

'Quite fortunate,' she managed, steeling herself to chew on a green adder with bright eye and visible tongue.

'I do hope it stays fine for the Great Meet next week,' offered Stritch.

'What Great Meet?' choked out Animal.

'Yes, haven't you heard? Next week Our Lady, Mama Shag is holding Annual Gathering here.'

Animal inclined her head indicating she would like to hear more. She was now more in command of herself and chewed another tough bite from the living adder Stritch offered her as moist chocolate gateaux.

'Yes Annual Gathering of the Pure Society of Shrinkers. You know, her respectable quasi-Christian ascetic sect. She is a most involved Shrinker. It really is quite hard to believe when you see that Hound Mahoney sucking lasciviously upon her genitalia. Funnily enough, she has a reputation for morals and virtue. A woman of parts. We, of course, will be gone by then.'

'Gone?' Animal choked on a snake's eye that had fallen out of its socket and into her throat.

'May I tempt you with a slice of peach, furry on the outside, smooth within? Watch juice pour over my fingers as I cut into it.'

Animal watched as Stritch took the most active of the snakes (white and orange) and - nameless horror! - with a sharp vegetable knife cut it through the middle. Animal could not sustain sufficient idea of it as peach to stop her eyes goggling at the sight of quantities of snake blood and guts disgorging in Stritch's hands. Her stomach heaved. He scratched the inside of his left wrist with the point of his knife, drawing a drop of blood. He pressed the tip into the small wound. He held his wrist over the obsidian pyramid upon the altar; blood oozed and trickled on to its sheer surface.

'You have many scars; did you make all the cuts yourself?' Animal took a piece of peach Stritch had prepared for her with the bloodied knife. It might as well have been a section of his tongue, the trouble she had chewing it. It was, as far as she could see, the tip of a large brown and red snake, the largest of the snakes Stritch had in his picnic hamper, but not nearly so large as the anaconda she now saw idling along the length of the window and curved round the back of the altar.

Stritch made three cuts upon his left shoulder. Animal saw his blood as heavenly spring water falling on the crystal floor. 'The anaconda will be happy,' she thought, 'if the room is full of water.' But what would she do, she worried, how would she breathe? She imagined her clothes clinging sodden to her flesh like an iron tunic, enclosing her, stifling her, stifling the rising emotions she felt for Mahoney Hound, stifling the maternal watchfulness aroused that morning when she woke and leant over to kiss him.

'Yes,' Stritch said simply, 'I have made most of these cuts, that is dear Animal, apart from those made by you.' He held the blade out to her and squeezed it between his fingers, cutting them. She was fearful as she took the knife. She saw Stritch's blood forming a puddle around her feet, as water. The imaginary water rose and she wanted to remove her shoes, so she might have a better chance of eventually floating. The picnic cloth was sodden now. Snakes slithered back into the refuge of the hamper.

'Some of your scars are old and deep. These here.' She pointed to his hecticly scarred wrist. 'How did you get them?'

Blissfully unaware of impending flood, Stritch handed her a gold rimmed tea cup and saucer containing a dark liquid. She had no idea what the liquid was. She had seen him cut the heads off three snakes, squeeze their vital juices into her cup, while blood poured from his wounds. She knew this might not be really happening. She had participated in horrendous acts in the Crystal Room before, only to find that they could not possibly have happened, for neither her body nor any other of the ritual participants bore the marks to back up memory. No. She was not sipping from a cup of snake juice with water rising all around, pleasing an expectantly loafing anaconda. This was probably not happening.

'These cuts?' Stritch flicked his fringe back carelessly. 'I've always had them.' He pegged up the snake basket and leant across to Animal. The floor dissolved in water; his mouth frothed with blood, thick and scarlet as womb food. She dropped her tea cup in astonishment; its contents spilt on her dress, she shuddered as if burnt, her nerves on edge, living pain screaming inside her, dislodging itself as a baby would when ripe for birth. She saw the magickal receptivity of the altar filling up with her pain. The obsidian sphere throbbed and grew, pulsating egg-like before it exploded, as her teacup did on reaching the floor. The smash of it relieved her, for it proved that the room could not be full of water and she would not drown.

She leant forward to accept a lovely kiss from Stritch's mouth. She knew the big snake would come and wrestle their joined bodies and win and each vertebra would release love's true colours and she would reach a vast space where sensual pleasure was the missing piece of perfection. In crimson, then neon mauve, brilliant stars spun in her head.

Stritch licked her ear. 'And you never knew my name. You were never even interested in my name. You didn't stop to think for five minutes all the time I was giving you pleasure.' Stritch gripped the small of her back in his square hands, strong with psychic power. 'You never asked me the name of my mother nor father. You didn't find out that I was brought up by my grandmother; it didn't matter to you. You only wanted me for one thing. And I only wanted you to want me for one thing.'

'Stritch.'

'And I wanted you, instead of all the cunts who tried to take a part of me. But they couldn't. It was always you. Always her.' Stritch sobbed on Animal's shoulder; she stroked the back of his greasy hair, picking out twigs, dead leaves and moss.

'Est, Est,' he sobbed.

'It's time Stritch,' Animal reminded him as shadows lengthened. With a thump a mud coloured bird was thrown on to the glass by an unexpected gust.

'It is time.'

Time for them to slide together for sexmagick. It was easy for their mobile spines to find the movement of each other. Easy for his sky bound nothingness, his thin dizzy asceticism. Easy for him, in this act of magick, to save them all from the sensual indulgence, and consequent decadence of which Beast had warned.

10.2   People Are Gardens

Stritch listened as the white door to the Crystal Room gently clicked shut behind him. He hesitated before deciding not to lock the door, as he had hesitated before deciding not to unroll the long black blind to cover the window. No, the night was black enough for any darkness he needed.

With clattering feet he chased Animal down the wide oak staircase. Playfully, he made part of the descent by banister. A nail caught his trouser; it ripped material and skin.

'That was the *most* imaginative and affectionate orgasm.' No secret charity hidden in Stritch's smile, no patronising oneupmanship corrupting his happiness.

'Sexmagick is good,' confirmed Animal.

It was dark on the stairs, but they knew their way blind. She walked barefoot; she'd finally taken her shoes off to help her float in the imaginary flood, before the anaconda *had* come and wrestled their bodies into closest contact.

They stood at the foot of the staircase, monumental mounds of oak furniture around them. They paid attention to their breath; Animal's smelt of lime. Every bit of Stritch smelt of roses however he abused his body. He was an old woman's dream come true. Stritch lifted his face, analysing the atmosphere of incense sodden *Ridelands*.

'How do you know,' resumed Animal 'that that was the most *anything* orgasm when you claim to remember nothing?' She teased him, tickled him, but her fingers came away sticky with blood; she licked them clean.

'My body has a mind of its own.' He sucked upon her neck.

'How original!' She stretched her neck to accept his caress.

'My body is instinctive like a dancer's, like Nijinsky's; I don't need to think. I move, I live, I feel. Come with me Animal; for I sense something important will happen tonight.'

Animal took his hand; they kissed. He held her buttocks to bring her to him. They magicko-sensually engaged as ideas lined up within them, to be transferred into energy of pure being.

Animal brought one leg up and wound it round his waist, hooking her heel over his prominent hip bone to hold him to her; he did the same. Each on one leg, mouth to mouth, they stood as one, at the crossroads of the ground floor corridors. A spacious hallway led in one direction to living room, drawing room, study and further through arched passages to the kitchen. In the other direction was smoking room, games room and the old ballroom which was still used on occasion for dancing, feasting and orgies. A shorter wide hall stretched from front door to the pillared entrance leading on to the lawn and beyond to natural meadowland, a mellow view of the elusive grace of life ever changing, lots of sky always the big sky, meadows, and wood pigeons cooing their common refrain. By the humble door to the scullery was the kitchen garden with its harmonious rows of cabbages all year round.

Stillness surrounded interwined acolytes Stritch and Animal, forming a perfect counterpoise of balance as each stood on one leg to form a two-legged creature; Stritch, the one who bleeds and Animal, the one who has been bled. White gauze folded out from the back of their necks to the high hall ceiling, stickier and less visible than spider's web. This was astral gauze, an ethereal trap to attract The Beast.

The grand outside door between pillars opened and Mama Shag appeared holding a burning rush torch high above her head, her eyes blindfolded. There was a sudden inrush of air as a spiritual entity used Mama's energy to manifest, first it was gauzy white and indistinct. Slowly the entity emerged and massed within the web that stretched above Animal and Stritch as they mated sexmagickally. Beast appeared at first as a translucent ghostly cliché with flickering angelic wings.

'Speak. I am here. I, whom you have summoned.' Ferocious deep bellied barking in duet erupted as in leapt two black hounds with eyes of liquid fire, total irises pure red.

Footsteps tripped in the torchlight. 'Damn these stairs. Why they can't light them I shall never know.' Mahoney put a hand to the banister and made his way downstairs.

'Animal! Lillian!' he called, in such an ordinary voice! What was he trying to prove? 'I thought you said…we were… going away…' He bumped into the stalk-like mating couple. 'Lillian?' Aghast as if a major breach of a commitment was taking place. 'Lillian? It is you. Why don't you answer me? Lillian. Why don't you look at me? Is there no rushing ocean of animal need in your heart for a faithful battered mate? I know I am battered - not even the devil himself would recruit me to be amongst his number. I do not blame you. I do. I do blame you. Lillian!' he roared. 'Why can't you be ordinary? For me, an ordinary man. I have found the mystery I have pursued so long and now I wish to be ordinary. What irony! What tragedy! What poetry!'

A partially embodied voice called out, a voice that poured into ears as sand into an egg timer. 'You have all come and I am pleased.'

Awkwardly Mahoney realised he was naked. Terror seized his body and threw him two feet into the air. Stritch and Animal fell apart, flopping post-orgasmically to the floor.

Mama Shag wielded a leather hammer, swung it with two arms and struck a large brass gong etched with a green mandala, a series of sixteen paisley shaped segments forming a circle, each a different colour. The gong's sonic vibrations shook a glass case containing a stuffed owl; this tumbled off the wall into a gloomy corner where the glass shattered, leaving dead owl to rot at last.

Mahoney had thought he'd seen a ghost before, but he was not prepared for this grimaceless entity.

'I have come and all is well.' Beast's astral form announced.

'Who are you?' stammered out Mahoney.

'Who am I? I would cackle if I could. I would laugh in your face. Your whole body vibrates with the knowledge of who I am! You are here to join me, to become one of mine as these are, these you see fallen around my feet even when my feet are nowhere to be seen. Come and take your place.'

'No, never.' Poor Mahoney was way out of his depth.

'You have already come to me. Hound. Hound of Hell. Come and obey your Beast. It is rare for me to thrive on this earth and I am glad now I am here and alive. I digress. Hound of Hell, resume your natural form.'

Mama Shag's gong sounded again, three short notes, and a fire-eyed black hound leapt from Mahoney's body. Beast's 15 strong hunting pack was now complete. Mahoney took the place of Beast's fifth hound who had recently met an untimely end. This consolidated Beast's power and his human form flickered into focus. He scratched Mahoney Hound No.5 under his thick leather collar; Hound No.5 snarled.

The Beast held his ringed fingers palms together in front of his nose, drawing all present energy to his third eye in furious concentration. He absorbed all energy and a purple strand of astral light formed above his head. He stretched his arms out and light flashed from them. The Hound that had been Mahoney snatched a quick look, almost human in its pathos, at the inert Animal erotically entwined with inert Stritch. Then true to his new found dog nature he ran through the open door and out into the night.

'My Animal, you have done well!' The Beast congratulated. 'It was good to meet you here tonight. You may come to me soon. Do not give in to romantic expectations and all will be well. I leave you with bread and wine.' He placed two small packages by the bodies. 'How these children need shows! And who am I to disappoint the younger generation?'

The mumbling uncertain man of later middle age had been replaced by a tower of dynamic positivism. Mama Shag launched three fireworks upon the lawn; they exploded into clusters of stars.

'I return to Pet. We will complete.' Beast summoned an extra electro-magickal charge from Stritch and Animal who twitched and struggled for breath. 'We will complete.'

Beast's body was sucked away by an atmospheric vortex. Gradually his form lost its opacity and became dancing particles of smoky air that gathered speed to become the transparent essence of speed itself. He sped back to Pet, his favourite Hound of Hell, where his spirit body re-entered its physical form.

10.3 Animal Tranquillised? Mahoney Tranquil?

Animal padded across the floorboards with a glass of water and a phial of opium. She wore a long white wrap tied with a golden silk sash. The brown hair she usually pushed back from her face, was arranged in a neat pleat with trailing locks coiled flatteringly upon her cheeks. She had plucked her eyebrows into thin arches, drawn kohl around her eyes, painted her lips scarlet. On her feet were Roman style sandals with straps criss-crossing up her calves and tied behind her knees, in the soft patch where she smelt of peaches and sunset. She was underdressed for the time of year, early October, but she'd lost that deprived child starved look that went with her black sprigged frock.

She exuded tranquillity and success as she placed the medicine on the black and gold papier-mâché Chinese piece they used as a bedside table. She perched beside the sleeping Mahoney Hound on the bed where it stood abandoned in the middle of the room, abandoned by Animal; she hadn't slept there last night but in Mama Shag's dressing room. Mama Shag had had a large muffin supper before bed whereas Animal hadn't eaten a bite since her snaky tea with Stritch in the Crystal Room the previous day.

'Ssh.' She stroked Mahoney Hound's forehead with a cool white hand. 'Ssh.' His eyes flickered open, saw her and his pupils grew wide with fear. She smiled and he passed through his fear, as he had done last night. He relaxed.

'Ssh. Drink this and rest today. Stritch will bring you food later. You won't be seeing me again, maybe not ever; I'm going away to join Beast.'

Mahoney Hound No.5 was quiet and obedient. Didn't want to talk or beg her not to go. Didn't want to fall in love with her nor persuade her to stay with him forever, monogamous and ordinary. Beyond the knowledge of his heart, he had found equanimity and a sense of future. He now knew he was Hound No.5, one of the 15 Hounds of Hell and that the other 14 Hounds and His Master, The Beast, were his true companions. Who knew what Animal was? Or could understand her magickal relationship to Beast? He no longer wanted to revenge himself on Drummond, the man behind Beast, for what he had done to Animal. No, he wanted to do all he could to help Beast in his unique work.

This meditation faded to blissful quietude as the opium took effect. The sun began to bleed its goodbyes all over the bed and Animal was glamorous. No longer hounded by him, she was clean and cool with nerves of steel. He wanted to reach out and pull her to him; he hesitated, in awe of her.

'Better not,' she said, reading his thoughts. 'You've been through your second stage becoming and I'm not available to you in the same way. If you want love, sex, climax and heavenly limbs, you must hunt it down and make it your own. You can't have lovely sex as a result of the discoveries I have made about myself or because of what I am to Beast; you must find your own way.' She turned her back and waved a finger tip goodbye. Mahoney undressed her in his mind but he did not move from the bed to get hold of her. Sex had drifted from his body into his mind.

Chapter 11

11.1   Café Breakfast

'Why did I meet him and where did he go?' Est pushed the café door open with her shoulder. She and Claudia sat at a scruffy wooden table while Maltby ordered coffee, toast and marmalade, milk for Claudia.

'Mama who are you talking about?'

'A friend my dear.' She looked warmly into Claudia's eyes, to convey the intimacy she felt for this special person, this Stritch she yearned for with a fervour equal to her intense longing for The Magician.

'Have I met him?' Claudia cocked her head, thinking over people she knew.

'No you haven't. I've only met him twice.'

'Has he been to our flat?'

'Once. When you were asleep.'

'You should have woken me up.'

Maltby sat down and took Claudia's hand. 'My dearest girl, why meet Mr. Mystery when you have me at your beck and call?'

The breakfast arrived and Claudia hungrily bit into a piece of toast before even buttering it.

'You are hungry this morning dear Claudia.'

'Mr. Maltby I am always hungry.' Est gave her a disapproving look as a few toast crumbs tumbled on to the table as she spoke.

'Are you sure Stritch was a real person?' Maltby asked Est.

'How do you mean?'

'Your new persona has made you direct,' Maltby commented.

'Sorry. I'm all nerves this morning.' She drank down half a cup of milky coffee and leant back with closed eyes. Angular male body language came naturally to her, flirting didn't.

'Yeah, real enough.' She remembered their lovemaking on the forest floor. Real and near the core of herself creating emotions which had got into her painting. Landscapes reached out from green to mauve, into aquamarine, until land appeared as water, patterns inspired by the flow of liquid within her body. She and Stritch had been water flowing into water, upon the forest floor.

'He commands your thoughts?' asked Maltby sensitively.

'My thoughts, my dreams, my decisions, my painting.'

Maltby raised an eyebrow. 'The painting is exceptionally good. No chance of course, of selling it as an English woman here in London you know.'

'Luckily I am no longer an English *woman*.' Est smiled. A melancholic mind ramble about Stritch was a tonic to her.

Claudia laughed and banged the table with her hands. 'You're a man, a man man man!' Almost shouting. 'I want more food. I am ravenous.'

'You are always ravenous,' Maltby confirmed.

More toast was brought for Claudia.

'I have been saving this news Est,' Maltby lowered his voice. 'You know of course, that I took five of your paintings to Serge in Paris?' Est nodded. 'Well, do you want the good news or the superlative?'

She shrugged.

'Well, he liked the paintings very much, has already sold one. He is sad he couldn't get a higher price but it is always hard for unknown artists. He is sure that through his agency you will soon become known. He is longing to meet you.

'I am glad we will not need to present a female form; I know Serge. If he thought you female he would see the paintings differently. Instead of an exciting original expression of emerging genius, they would be the eccentric and chance production of one temporarily inspired with a passing interest in painting, not to be taken seriously. If he knew of your child why,' Maltby paused to take a look at a conspicuously eating Claudia, 'he would not want to shake your hand.

'With you a man and father, he will embrace your achievement in art and parenting. The price of success my dearest Est, is the price of a pair of trousers.' He squeezed her trousered knee underneath the small table. 'Whatever you do don't bed him; he propositions his artists, you know.'

Est had been half listening, drawn inward, thinking about Stritch and the feel of his body. Obsessively she went over their two encounters, reliving details repeatedly for accuracy. Raw, moody, unreconciled, ambiguous, he had taught her to mistrust herself, to doubt every emotion she felt, to question its authenticity. That her soul might have room to appear on the surface of her personality like the morning sun rising above the horizon.

'If the price of success is a pair of trousers,' Est resumed as they left the café, 'it comes cheap. Claudia found these with the rubbish on a side street.'

'Cheap and easy, destiny will carry you speedily along,' Maltby prophesised.

'I will absorb fear and become a monster,' Est declared, 'not as ugly as Frankenstein but ten times as scary. Will you still love me then my darling Claudia?'

'I will always love you Mama. You are the loveliest Mama in all the world.' The three held hands as they walked along the street.

'I'll try only to scare our enemies and they in their terror will run far away to the other side of the world where they will forget to hate me.'

'And we will have no enemies left,' rejoined Claudia.

'Exactly,' Est confirmed. She changed her voice. 'Darling Maltby, exalted among human beings for compassion, generosity and sensitivity.'

'At your service, noble genius.'

'You read me like a book.'

'Like a painting. I am better with images than words.' They walked the quickstep of happiness.

'Then you'll be pleased that I wish to spread my wings tonight.'

'One of your dates with fate?'

'How did you guess?' Est stopped and threw her arms about him, but pulled away as several passers by stared in astonishment. Of course she wore trousers and men didn't hug men in public in England. She laughed. 'I'll tell you where I'm going when I've been there.'

'It's not dangerous?' Maltby asked in a mock fatherly tone.

'No, I intend only to indulge the part of me that seeks comfort.'

'Don't invent a spell for raising the dead.' Maltby waited at Est's door. 'I won't come in; I'll be back tonight.'

'Ce soir, et demain?' asked Est.

'Paris!' All three chorused. Monsieur Serge had sent money for the painting, not a fortune but quite a lot of money if you were used to nothing, enough for a lot of breakfast and the initial stages of relocation.

11.2   Est Loves Stritch

'Stritch!' Est called to noone. She had a fairly long walk cross country before she reached the place that pulled her to itself, the river by Mama Shag's place, where she'd first met Stritch.

Her world was green-black, alive with wind-born leaves. The waning moon was still gibbous. 'Stritch.' His name commingled with movements of insect and bat in the invisible life of night. Falling birch leaves curved away from her mantra. 'Stritch.'

The path had been worn hollow by centuries of use. Cartwheels, hooves, feet, ploughshares and thrashers had all passed this way. Successive rainy autumns had seen earth churned to mud and thrown up either side of the way into two heaps of topsoil where grew straight ash, scrawny hawthorn and mysterious rowan.

Est's pace lengthened and her muscles warmed inside her trousers. Her hands cupped the air as she walked. She felt an intense need to satisfy inner self. She would never be content with a bit of company to nurse the hours of life. She needed to unite her passion and curiosity in one surge of vitality moving faster than the speed of city or country.

She sniffed the air. It smelt of Earth-sweat. Her impulse was to stay out in the night, until first sun made damp grass steam and then to race back to Maltby and Claudia in the liberty of trousers, with Stritch within her forever.

She smelt the river close by, pictured the hump back bridge and bank sloping down to the thorn tree where she had first seen him. Alive in her imagination, Stritch beckoned her. She broke into a run, staring through the shapes in the sky to the whites of *his* eyes. She opened her mouth in an exclamation of desire. She *knew* he was waiting for her. The world jogged up and down as she ran. There was a row of round stones beside the path and then the bridge came into view.

'Stritch,' she panted. She squinted into darkness asking, 'Is this the time and place?' Her breath steadied, 'Stritch!' Answered by several wing fluttering escapes from her vicinity and the small 'plop' of a stone thrown into the burbling river.

She clambered down the slope to her favourite predator and knelt eagerly beside him. Her heart beat loud in her throat forming one word only and that word part of herself, 'Stritch.' She recoiled as his lips curled into a fake smile. It was as if she beheld a mask portraying a mass of sores. Then the strange mask dropped and his usual sultry black and white searched her wistfully for assurance. He threw another pebble into the river. A mutual atmosphere of let-down. 'Stritch, you're here.' He nodded his assent and chucked another pebble. 'Did you have something you wanted to tell me? A moment ago you looked different.' He shrugged.

'Who was it? Who were you?' Est persisted.

His purple lips, fat with passion, moved to kiss her, to elicit her surrender.

She pulled away. 'Who were you? What were you trying to say?' He clasped his knees.

She put a finger out to a dark splodge on his white trousers. His face was angelic. 'You're bleeding.' She moved closer; her head tilted into kiss position. They closed their eyes. His lips were warm and sticky; his mouth was heaven undisputed, thoughtful, soulful, mouth of man.

Again she saw the mask of another man upon Stritch's face. 'The Magician,' she thought, the one she had been searching for when she'd found Stritch. She felt his soft neck skin. He was irresistible and simultaneously repulsive, but then his personality was obliterated as her vision of The Magician merged with their passion.

'It's funny,' she thought as they made love, 'how samey this is, the same as last time the same as the time before. First in the wood then in the flat and now here, I feel the same, as if there never can be a conversation between us.'

'I feel nothing for you,' Est said and currents of colour poured through her heart. Stritch dug his nails into her shoulders. The river flowed on; wings swept through the air and Est longed for an ordinary conversation, the exchange of biographical material, quiet private thoughts upon subject of politics, individuality and art. Her body taxied along the runway of orgasm.

Their sweat lay damp and cold within partially removed clothing. They shivered, appeased animals of nocturnal appetite.

'Paris,' mumbled Stritch hoarsely.

Est was taken aback; Paris? Where she, Maltby and Claudia were going tomorrow? Going for good. Was he going to, or had he come from Paris? Too many questions. She rested her head on his shoulder and sought no explanation or information.

'I love this place,' he said and coughed. 'Here, I found out that I am not what I was brought up to believe myself to be. I was not educated by my education, not dressed by my clothes nor nourished by the food my mother prepared for me.

'All the books I read were loaded with the shrapnel of lies. I sometimes imagine the inexcusable liars who wrote the lies all sitting before their desks, taking a white piece of paper. The writer smoothes the paper with the palm of his hand.' Stritch slunk up closer to Est. They were nose against nose; his hands on her back were damp and trembling. 'With a fountain pen he writes the date and title. He suppresses an initial urge to write, "Before the end of the world I will find my true love, even if that means forsaking pleasure forever." Instead he writes, "She occasionally wanted to believe in her own destiny; such immature yearning would briefly preoccupy her, but she had come to understand that the art of living was the art of compromise, compromise and diplomacy; she was extremely satisfied with her marriage."

'If instinct were already dead in this writer of lies I could forgive him.' Stritch paused to stretch his neck. 'Est, your name? Unusual. Did your mother name you that?'

Est felt a spasm of triumph; he had asked the first direct question. She didn't reply but stared into the petrol blue ribbon of water.

'I must go. I've got to walk home.'

'I'll come with you,' he offered. They rose together in one elegant movement.

'Shall we walk through the dark woods together?' She smiled in reply and took his cold hand. There were many questions unasked and unanswered between them.

'I like your trousers and your haircut. You look like a man.'

'If you grew your hair and wore a cream coloured frock, you'd be the perfect girl.' Est fondled his wasted pectorals as if they were breasts. He pushed his chest forward and wriggled girlishly.

'I don't want to wear cream; too nice and ordinary. If I wore a dress it would be deep purple and silky.'

They were walking fast, away from the city.

'We're going the wrong way.' Est stopped. 'I must go home.'

She didn't recognise the path in the dark. She was worried about getting back to Claudia.

'We're not going home.' Stritch threw maximum contempt upon the word "home". 'We're going to Mama's. Come on.' He gripped her arm and ran. She had to comply. Claudia was with Maltby who would not worry for a few hours yet. It wouldn't be too long 'til morning. They ran to Mama, the cavern and night ritual.

Stritch led Est down the six white steps and knocked upon a door of old yew reinforced with rusted iron.

He rapped on the door and had a fit of coughing before managing to call, 'Mama!' No reply; he turned the door handle to lift a latch and pushed the heavy door open. Dew and moss fell upon his head. He pulled Est into the passageway. 'Ssh.'

Est noticed he had a half-healed cut on his swollen left eyelid, the eye was nearly closed. Why hadn't she noticed that before?

'I'm not sure that I want to be here,' she said as incense of cinnamon and jasmine wafted through the earth walled corridor where two torches burnt.

'I need to eat; I don't know where I am, I need to get back to Claudia.'

'Ssh, can you hear?' A humming, like many bees. 'Hear that?'

'Yes, I can, but..?' replied Est uneasily.

Stritch held her elbow firmly. 'You should come with me now, into this cavern, you will be surprised how very little time will pass.' His eyes were inhumanly mauve, shining as if they let out light manufactured within.

Est, impressed, nodded humbly and complied.

11.3   Death

Two, three, four steps into the passageway and a golden curtain shimmered before them. Cymbals clashed and slid, one upon another. Brighter light than that in the earth passage flickered around the edges of the curtain which was then drawn back from inside by an invisible agent. A voice proceeded from the chamber, deep yet feminine:

> 'You can hear and you can smell
> But you cannot see and you cannot touch.'

A chorus of undifferentiated voices recited:

> 'You cannot see, though you are not blind.
> You cannot hear, though you are not deaf.'

> 'A great battle has been fought,' resumed the leader.
> 'The righteous have been overthrown,
> The world is ruled by traitors.'

Voices hissed and crackled at Est like scrambled radio stations, while her navel radiated colour generated by her heart.

> 'Your body is the traitor ruling your world!' continued the leader.
> A great gong reverberated and Est rocked within a tidal wave of sound.
> The chorus chanted:

> 'Forsake your body,
> A traitor cannot guarantee security.

Forsake your personality,
The betrayed are the carriers of brutality.

Eliminate desire,
Beauty's origin is eternal fire.'

Perfumed smoke filled the chamber. Stritch coughed once, twice, small dry coughs, thrice and he floundered. His feet seemed too small for balance, his head too huge to be upheld by his neck. Arms flopped at his sides as he fell.

'His time has come.' Mama Shag's deep voice implied evil neutralised through her agency.

'Choice was his illusion,' Mama, The Lady of The House, continued and smoke soaked up echo. 'Choice has brought him back to the crossroads; the journey has changed him beyond recognition. He has not the strength to run fast beneath the arch where the predators of the past lurk.'

'He dies for us,' hissed the chorus and their robes swished this way and that. Est felt as if plasma was being drained from pipes plugged into her arteries under anaesthetic. In sleeplike trance she did not notice the chorus nail Stritch upon a yew crucifix and erect it behind the altar. Blood poured from his nail wounds.

New liquid, of extra terrestrial origin flowed into Est's body. She re-entered mundane consciousness and pearl light radiated from her mouth; she drooled drops of mauve elixir. 'Eternity,' she uttered and opened her eyes.

She found she was lying on a thin white sheet spread upon the floor of the otherwise empty cavern; even the altar had been removed. Stritch lay beside her on the floor, his face brown with dried blood, mouth and eyes locked open. Flies buzzed around him.

Est screwed up her nose; fear's diarrhoea marked his forest stained white trousers. His naked feet had been violently fore-shortened. There, on the stumps where his feet had been attached, maggots crawled. 'Already,' she whispered. Very little remained of his eyeballs; his eye sockets were a seething mass of blowfly larvae. While she was immaculate! Manicured hands and feet, hair washed and combed and she was dressed in a new silk shirt with her tweed trousers.

Horrified, she gawped at Stritch, so recently her love and part of her projected future, Paris and all.

To her great surprise, in came Mama Shag and Lillian bearing a coffin. Workmanlike, they placed the coffin down next to the body, rolled the white sheet around him and chatted through the best way to get him into the coffin.

Est was dumbfounded at their matter-of-fact demeanour. 'Where were the police?' She wondered. 'Surely he could not have hacked off his own feet?' A wave of nausea came over her as she remembered that Stritch had been cut down from the crucifix while still alive. That with his dying breath he had hacked off his own feet while people stood and watched, herself included - had watched as he'd died.

Mama Shag and Lillian removed the golden sashes from their waists and their silk robes fell loose. They passed their sashes under Stritch's wrapped body, securing the bundle with neat knots. They gestured Est to participate. Awkwardly she untied her golden sash and wrapped it around Stritch's waist.

The coffin was lined with pearl silk and strewn with red rose petals. The three women lowered shrouded Stritch carefully, reverently, into the coffin. Est took her shirt off and wrapped his dismembered feet in the silk (warm from her body), and placed them in the coffin.

'Claudia,' thought Est as Lillian and Mama Shag left the chamber; a whole line of rainbow coloured curtains closed behind them.

'Claudia.' She groped through the curtains which clung to her face, inhibiting her movement. With great effort she passed through the last curtain and with relief found herself before the yew door to the outside world. Mama Shag had locked it. Est looked through the keyhole. It was dark outside; she had a few hours yet before her absence would worry Maltby. He was probably asleep upon her bed and would not awaken before Claudia.

11.4   Underground Glamour

'If only he had waited for the world to wake up.' Est turned from the locked door and faced a diaphanous lilac curtain which blew against her hair. Nausea in her stomach, translucent colours in her mind, thought organised to one side. Est blundered through the curtain into a passage curving off to the left. Mama Shag and Lillian had extinguished the torches and the passage was dark. Est dreamt awake: she could not see but was not blind.

The tunnel was cool; she had a strong urge to remove her shoes and feel Earth with bare feet. She wore men's brown Oxfords; Claudia had found them with the male clothes. They'd stuffed cut up cloth into the toes as they were two and a half sizes too big. She took the shoes off; they smelt of someone else's feet and were creased with someone else's stride; she tied them together by their laces. She swung the shoes and let the laces slip through her fingers and fall to the ground; did not pause to recover them.

She walked easily and fast. The tunnel inclined; Est licked her lips and tasted salt. She came to an obstruction entirely filling the passageway. Her 3D sight returned but she could see little.

The tunnel was full of green shadows and thin air; hard panic rose in Est's throat. From outside came the rumble and almighty crash of thunder. Within the tunnel she came upon an unexpected barrier and tore the palm of her hand on a nail sticking out from wood. She calmed her mind, to enable methodical function. 'For surely,' she thought, 'this obstruction has to be a door.' She found a handle but no keyhole, only hinges and two more sharp nails.

Her feet were cold and getting colder; she stood first on one foot then the other, rubbed the soles of her feet against the back of her calves. Her stomach rumbled; it was empty as empty could be. She was thirsty. She heard voices on the other side of the door but could not make out words.

She stood before the door, wanting to be back with Claudia. Unsure what to do, telling herself there was a way out, she didn't want to retrace her steps.

Avoiding nails she pushed the door with her shoulder and then harder with all her considerable strength. The door gave way suddenly; Mama Shag had unlocked it from the other side and stood by expectantly as Est arrived in the kitchen; the room was cheerful with firelight and the smell of baking.

Wordlessly Mama Shag handed her a pair of grey shoes with high heels and a buttoned strap. While Est put the shoes on, Mama Shag towel-dried Est's wet hair and combed it as one would a child's, murmuring soothing words. Lillian handed Est a cup of warm cocoa and covered her shoulders with a shawl.

'In a moment,' said Lillian, 'I am going to dress you in a beautiful silk dress. You will feel distinguished and look glamorous. You are one of us, independent and free. Your name is...'

'I don't want to wear a fine lady's costume. I am a painter. I have a name.' Est impatiently broke from the hairbrush and tottered on heels. 'Claudia,' she thought and 'home.'

Outside the warm kitchen the daytime sky was thunderstorm dark; insistent vertical rain drummed on the roof. 'Home.'

'Shall I drive her home?' Lillian asked Mama Shag/Our Lady.

'If she won't wear the dress, I doubt if she'll ride in the car,' Our Lady replied.

'Are you very wealthy?' Est asked.

Our Lady snorted. 'Wealthy, tosh! We are filthy rich.'

'Oh god, Stritch! Where is he?'

Lillian and Mama Shag exchanged a conspiratorial "Shall we

tell her?" look.

'I'll drive you home,' offered Lillian. 'I'll put on my driving robe.'

Est wrapped herself in a shawl.

'Shan't you wait until the rain has stopped?' asked Our Lady.

'Oh no,' Lillian said casually, rummaging in a cupboard and selecting a grey tweed jacket with matching hat. 'At your service rain or shine.' She saluted and pulled one of her big hungry grins, lips stretching to the corner of her eyes. 'Animal do not linger; we must pack your bags.'

'I shall not linger, I shall not dally, I shall take the lady home and I shall return, sir.' She saluted again, her face sinister.

'Did Stritch write any poetry?' Est asked Animal as they boarded Mama's huge car. 'Poetry? He doesn't know how to write his own name.'

Est absorbed this like a punch in the stomach. It would be good to be with Claudia and Maltby, share a meal and converse. It occurred to Est that Stritch might not be dead. The roar of the engine pleased her and appeased her curiosity. After all she didn't know him well, didn't know him at all. She felt him and that was a different thing altogether. If he was dead he died for a cause, some weird sect and their minority belief system.

'Christ what a car!' Est thought as they purred along in the thin morning light. Thick clouds obstructed the sun. The wind had risen and drove rain hither and thither erratically as they approached the medieval city's north gate.

Animal pulled up outside Est's flat; Claudia's smudged face could just be discerned, pressed to the basement window pane, watching out for her Mamma. Animal got out and opened the door for Est, chauffeur style, but barefoot. She tipped her cap. 'Until Paris.' Animal was on fire with an exhilaration that was not really to Est's taste.

'Paris,' concurred Est.

Chapter 12

12.1   Blood Stains

'Last night I had a dream, do you understand, a dream for a nation.'

'Yes Animal my dear, I understand.' Mama Shag blew her nose loudly upon a large checked handkerchief, approaching a tea towel in size. She rubbed Animal's back vigorously. 'I'll drive you to the station soon; your train leaves in 45 minutes. I must prepare for The Shrinkers. Are there any strange smells in the house to expel? Let us polish the Ballroom floor while you tell me your dream.' The Shrinkers, short for The Pure Society of Shrinkers, was Mama's other, respectable sect. They espoused little philosophy and much belief, centred on asceticism.

'Your house smells of candles and blood,' confided Animal as the two women pushed open the oak doors to the ballroom.

'Blood!' exclaimed Mama Shag.

'Yes, a saint's blood.' The two kneeling women applied polish to the floor beneath the long banqueting table upon which lay the coffin, decorated with a single red rose.

'Will The Shrinkers appreciate this coffin in their midst?' asked Animal.

'You are taking it to Paris with you.'

'What!'

'Yes. It has been cleared with the relevant authorities. I have the report from the asylum where Stritch was before he came here. It confirms that they feared for his life, that he had repeatedly attempted suicide, self-mutilated and rarely ate. It concludes with a life expectancy of six months, given one year ago.

'Beast will meet you in Paris where you will help him finalise funds and from there proceed to Cefalù where Our Order will truly be born.'

'You say "Our Order". Will you join us?' Animal vigorously polished out a stain.

'No, I will provide certain funds. Miss Jane, who will be joining you, will supply the remainder.'

'A Shrinker to the end.'

'Of course.'

'We Thelemites are your hobby.'

'More than that. The 93 Current is my life blood. Come Animal. Scott and Marty are waiting to take the coffin.'

'Are they coming too?'

'Can you shoulder a coffin? I have packed you a small case. Be swift.' Mama Shag patted Animal's bottom in a motherly way to hurry her up the stairs. She sniffed; did the air really smell of blood? She'd have to spread the smell of cooking bread while singing a requiem for Stritch, she thought. She had loved him; she blew her nose. She was in love with him. He banished inhibition; he belonged to wood and river. Insane? She snorted; she thought not.

Mama Shag pounded a large lump of dough, turned it and pressed the heels of her hands into its increasing elasticity. Pleased with its smooth, slightly sticky mass she returned it to the big bowl, put a damp tea towel over it and left it by the stove to rise.

The front door bell rang; she quickly washed her hands and ushered the first Shrinkers into her cosy private sitting room on the first floor of the East Wing, apologising for a small wait while she drove her "niece" to the station.

12.2   Animal's Departure

Marty and Scott were somewhat unbrushed. Marty's trousers were too short and Scott's noticeably too tight. The clothes brush had been used on their fronts but not their backs where they could not see; there every bit of fluff showed on their black suits.

'Why Lillian dearest, you look beautiful,' said Mama Shag admiringly. Indeed she did. Ladylike and properly dressed in heeled shoes, silk stockings, camiknickers, an under slip, a knee length black crepe long sleeved dress, nicely tailored with a high neck and matching short jacket. A black wool cape was neatly folded over the small brown suitcase that Mama Shag had packed for her.

Marty and Scott hoisted the coffin as they would a bale of animal fodder or fertiliser, their usual cargo during their work round Mama's estate. Awkwardly, they clambered into the back of the car, hauling the coffin across their knees. One of the back doors would not shut and had to be secured with a rope. They were obliged to travel slowly to the station out of respect for the dead and receive salutes along the way. They arrived at the station after the train was due to leave.

Fortunately the guard was holding the train for them; Mama Shag was as royalty in the neighbourhood, much loved for her sensitive charity. No one suspected that she had an unusual, ceremonial, private life. People merely assumed that she had many friends she liked to invite to stay, particularly since the death of her beloved husband.

Mama Shag quickly arranged for the coffin to be stowed in the guard's van. Mama Shag closed the train door upon Animal calling, 'Goodbye you wonderful creature.' Then the guard blew his whistle and the glamorous locomotive sighed in preparation, before pulling out of the station.

Animal smiled enigmatically and raised a gloved hand for an understated farewell. Her sylphlike form was elegant in the delightful outfit Mama Shag had provided.

Mama Shag took out the big hanky and wiped her nose as the train gathered speed. Animal, with Scott and Marty to assist as needed, would take the coffin to London from where they would take the boat train to Paris. She thanked the stationmaster warmly for delaying the train's departure for her party.

'Now Annual Gathering, prayer and compassion,' Mama told herself. She felt nostalgic for her brief flowering while with Stritch and felt his loss acutely.

12.3   Train Sex Ritual

Marty and Scott secured the coffin safely in the guard's van. Once the train was well on its way, they decided to wait on Animal. They knocked on her first class compartment door.

'Come in!' she called with a voice as light and teasing as feather down.

Once in her compartment the two fellows coughed into their hands, unused to wearing gloves. Awkwardly, they looked downwards and shuffled their feet. 'We wondered,' said Scott.

'That is, we wondered if we could do anything to make you comfortable,' completed Marty.

'One of you must stay with the coffin. The other I would like to sit beside me, as I do not wish to be alone.'

'No of course not, of course not,' agreed Scott. He coughed nervously as he backed out of the compartment and exchanged a worried look with Marty. He could not imagine himself sitting beside this exotic creature; he'd heard rumours about her too. And now he couldn't take his eyes off her lips, he was relieved to be out in the corridor.

'Please draw the curtains,' Animal ordered Marty who duly obliged, blacking out the corridor on one side and passing autumnal scenery on the other.

'Place my cloak about my shoulders. I am cold.'

'Like that, m'lady?' asked Marty.

'Not m'lady,' corrected Animal.

'What shall I call you?' Marty sat one seat away from Animal with his feet square upon the floor. He had on light fawn socks which did not go with the black suit.

'We shall see what you shall call me as the journey progresses.' Animal closed her eyes. 'Have you ever kissed a girl?' Her voice was as light as the touch of a feather. One silk clad leg crossed upon another revealed silk knees.

'Yes of course I have.'

'Yes, yes,' interrupted Animal impatiently. 'I mean really kissed her, every part of her. Felt what her most intimate lips feel like, taste like. Have you licked her?'

A knock on the door, 'Tickets, please.'

Animal handed the ticket collector three first class tickets provided for them by Mama Shag.

'Have you?' reiterated Animal, when the conductor had left their compartment.

No answer.

'Would you like to now?'

No answer.

'Sit opposite me,' commanded Animal, making it easy for Marty. 'Look at me.' She stood slowly, deliberately and took off her silk lace-edged camiknickers and laid them neatly on the seat beside her. The movement of the train nudged the knickers along the seat; soon they would slide off.

Animal sat down and eased her dress up to her thighs. As she lifted it, she opened her black silk clad thighs. Her dress reached the line of her stocking tops.

'Look at me.'

Marty choked, 'I can't take my eyes off you.'

Animal languidly traced the opening of her vaginal lips with a moistened finger.

The handle of the door turned and in came Scott.

'Sorry,' he mumbled.

'No, come in, join us,' insisted Animal. 'You can either watch or participate.' The men were meekly in awe of her.

'Kneel before me Marty, with your head between my thighs.' Marty quickly removed his hat and did as he was told. His warm hair stroked her thighs.

'Kiss me, as if you were kissing my mouth. Open my lips with your lips, run your tongue inside, find a way in. Do not be satisfied until you have kissed me to utter abandon.'

Marty's tongue found her vaginal opening and he moved his lips upon her pussy, nuzzling her clitoris fervently. She laughed and curled her pelvis up; her knees fell apart opening more, for Marty to kiss more completely.

'Scott come here. Closer. Can you see how Marty kisses? I want you to pleasure me. Did you know that a woman often likes her anus stimulated?

'Well, I…'

'I do. Kneel on the floor and put your finger in my arse. Don't you want to pleasure me, Scott?'

'It's not that.'

'Would you rather suck my nipples, roll you tongue around my soft rosy buds?'

'Well, I…'

'Or would you rather lay me down full length upon this seat and shag me with that hard rod of passion I see rising unmistakably within your trousers, until I beg you to stop and beg you never to stop simultaneously?'

'Well I…'

'Thank you Marty. Do you know what Marty has done Scott? Marty has put his finger in my anus. I believe I've found out what you want.' Lillian changed position, to kneel up upon the seat facing the backrest, her dress pulled up, her white buttocks marked with whip welts, enticingly laid bare.

'Show Scott what you were doing, Marty.' Animal pulled her buttock cheeks open while Marty put one, then two fingers in her anus and unbuckled his trousers with his free hand.

'Do you think he's going to shag my anus Scott? Is he brave enough for that? What do you think? Or will you take over? Are you disgusted with me?'

'Yes I am, as a matter of fact.'

'In that case Scott, open my case. You'll find a whip. Feel free to express yourself. I will take up position for my punishment. I must be punished.'

Scott had opened the case and found the leather lash. He fondled its flexible length, glad that there was this way to express the excitement he felt uncomfortable with.

'Marty, take your finger out of my anus. Good, your trousers are undone. You are a lovely boy aren't you? Lie down on your back while I mount you and present my wicked buttocks to your disgusted work mate.'

Scott, red in the face and furious at himself because he couldn't take his eyes from her silky vaginal lips, moist and pink, descending upon Marty's joyous erection. He was relieved to cut into her buttocks hard, with the knot, and again hard as he could, lifting her dress to bare her skin and avoid Marty's scrotum. He could see his friend's testicles tremble as semen surged within them. But it was the sight of Animal's blood he found finally irresistible.

His actions were totally out of character as he mounted her anus. 'Just like an animal,' he told himself as he unfastened his belt and button and got on top of her even while she sat upon Marty's cock and rode him. Scott pushed right up into her anus and was glad that it made her cry out and glad that her cry was a cry of pain. He thrust harder as she cried out again.

Marty was rock hard under her; aroused by Scott's frenzy he

was coming into her cunt as Scott was getting ready to ejaculate into her arse, an act he'd thought he'd never perform.

After masculine passion had peaked, Animal slipped out from between the two of them and sat demurely upon the seat. She wriggled and giggled and met their eyes with her own.

'Pass me my knickers Scott.' Exhausted and disgusted with himself, Scott still obeyed the voice of authority. Animal slipped into her knickers and politely looked away as the boys tidied themselves.

'While we travel,' she commanded, 'I need sexual titillation. I hope you understand. Whether it be the whip, a hand upon my genitals or whatever. I hope neither of you tires easily.' Animal stroked the fingers of her soft grey gloves. 'From now on, one of you must stay with the coffin at all times. Do you understand?'

'Yes of course,' the boys mumbled guiltily, 'sorry, we...'

'I will overlook your misbehaviour this once; it must not be repeated.'

Marty and Scott exchanged looks, soundlessly deciding who should stay with sex goddess Scarlet Woman and who should guard the coffin. It was Scott, the initially reluctant who stayed with Animal. He liked the whip. He liked her bleeding bottom and the rest, the anal intercourse.

Chapter 13

13.1 Another Train to Paris

'You think my pictures will sell in Paris?' Est asked Maltby. The movement of the train swung her against Claudia who sat between Maltby and her mother. They were travelling second class.

'They have already sold; it is more a question of your continuing to work, to develop your direction.' Maltby wore a cream suit. Est still dressed as a man looked the part, if a bit round about the buttocks.

'My new direction! Painting is a compulsion for me. I cannot stop; it is the business side that stumps me. Dearest Maltby, how grateful I am to you!'

'Why are you grateful to him Est?' asked Claudia bouncing up and down in her seat, overjoyed to be travelling by train and later by boat!

'Please keep still my darling, I'm sure the springs of these seats were not designed to be bounced upon,' Est advised soberly.

'You always spoil my fun.'

'If I spoil your fun, why am I taking you in this train and across the sea to live a new, exciting life in Paris?'

'Alright I suppose you don't spoil my fun. Play with me Est. Play with me Maltby, tell me a story.'

'I'll read you a fairy tale,' Est suggested.

'No, I want one of your stories,' insisted Claudia, eyes gleaming.

'I can't turn my imagination on at will; I have a lot on my mind.'

'You always have a lot on your mind.'

'What about *The Princess and The Pea, Jack and The Beanstalk*, or *Beauty and The Beast?*'

'Not *Beauty and The Beast!*' Claudia's least favourite story.

'You like *The Princess and The Pea.*'

'I don't want *The Princess and The Pea.* I want a made up story. You tell me one Maltby, please.' She clutched his sleeve and cuddled up to him.

'I'll tell you a story from my own imagination,' agreed Maltby.

'Can it be about the goblin called Hamlin and the leprechaun called Libel?'

'They may come into it; the star of the piece is a hobgoblin called Razzmatazz who at the beginning of the story had no friends at all and no family.'

Claudia snuggled closer.

'Razzmatazz was called Razzmatazz solely because his entire body was jazzy red. No elf, sprite or goblin knew where this colour had come from for no one else had it, only Razzmatazz. Sadly neither his body colour nor name suited him for he was a gloomy fellow, true to the nature of all hobgoblins. Gloomy and inclined to mischief. He was not satisfied if a day went by and he had not put the spanner into someone's works.'

The rhythm of Maltby's voice blended with the sway of the train; little sleep the previous night meant Claudia soon could not keep her eyes open. She fought sleep, wanted to stay awake for the story; sleep gently won the battle. She slumped upon Maltby's shoulder; he put an arm about her to prevent her falling off the seat.

For a while Maltby and Est sat in silence. The train was comparatively empty, they had chosen to travel at this late hour, knowing it would be quiet. One elderly gentleman sat in an opposite corner, hidden behind a large newspaper; he was all hat and trousers.

Est and Maltby watched the passing scenery. It did not take long to get out of their city, being still largely confined to its medieval boundaries. Arable farmland with brown fields ploughed into glossy earth clods followed. Petrol grey clouds rolled across copse and hedgerow. It was an hour and a half before the scenery became urban again and larger towns came close together with golf courses and allotments inbetween.

Est was first to stir. 'He had marks all over his body. The soft place behind the knee, even there, as if he had deliberately sought out the most tender places to mutilate. Why would he do that?'

'You're talking about Stritch again?'

'Of course I am,' snapped Est. Maltby made a pantomime face of recoil at her outburst.

'I'm sorry to snap. I saw him die and felt the most delicate ecstasy. A gourmet emotion, as far from sensuality as true pleasure really is. He had such virtue.'

'And artistic talent no doubt,' Maltby added in commemoration of Stritch - phantom lover, bloody exhibitionist, reclusive icon.

'Such talent.'

'Almost matches you know who,' winked Maltby.

'Quite,' agreed Est and laughed with relief. 'If there is no battle,' she continued inspired, 'between disparate elements, each factor added to say, a piece of music will be isolated and discordant. Battle is a statement of coexistence implying chaos, for juxtaposition insures that the listener's attention has no fixed point and will experience harmony.

'Though for all the efforts of my mind I still cannot explain why Stritch turned against himself completely.'

'Are you sure he is dead?'

'I saw him die. I suppose I may have been dreaming. It *was* ecstasy.'

'He may not be dead,' reasserted Maltby.

'Equally, he may never have been alive.'

'Really?'

'Oh no, no. This is all talk. I saw him crucified!' Est moaned.

'Surely not?'

'That was what I saw. Two women, one young and one old, nailed him to a cross using heavy iron hammers.'

'Yet before you said it was suicide?'

'Yes, I'm sure about that. He was already dead when he was

nailed upon the cross. If he hadn't been dead then he was very close to death when Mama Shag and Animal nailed him to the cross.'

'In that case they killed him,' argued Maltby.

'Whatever they would do, they would not kill him. Not even if The Beast commanded it and I don't think he would do that. Manipulation of another's Will is not what he's about.

'Stritch had a highly developed Will,' she continued. 'However, his intelligence had been developed before his Will. He had become a series of ideas connected to the idea of "self" as an object. Upon his body, removed from sensuality, he exerted his Will. This was a betrayal for he did not care what he did to his body. Self sacrifice had become self indulgence. He could no longer detect truth amongst the lies in which we all live.' Est's cupid bow lips pouted.

'I don't altogether follow you.' Maltby looked askance.

'You don't need to follow me now. I'm sure to go on and on and on about this until you're begging me to stop. I'll call on you to rescue me from this tragedy in the middle of many frightening nights. You won't be able to provide even minimal comfort. I shall blame you for this pain that only Stritch could relieve.'

'You seem to have made up your mind to be hopeless,' offered Maltby. He took a flask of whisky from his pocket and offered it to Est; she gratefully took a swig.

'It isn't my mind that's made up. If it was my *mind* I could formulate an escape from misery. It's not my body that hurts either, it's my soul.'

'A disease of the soul you seem to have inherited from Stritch, to use pain and betrayal as a way of coping with life's incongruence.' Maltby drank whisky and offered it again to Est.

'A drop more,' she winked.

Claudia's eyes flickered open briefly, before the beautiful rocking momentum took her back to deep sleep.

'To resume. Did he mention any family?' Maltby asked.

'He never talked of anything but "the moment". The atmosphere he generated strongly focussed everybody around him entirely upon "the moment". It was intoxicating and disorientating; this was his fascination. It was as if he had no life before the "moment" and no memory of previous personal encounters, except for a growing degree of person-specific warmth. A rising heat, if you will.'

'He must have had a mother and father, a schooling and the rest.'

'A schooling, yes I suppose, though come to think of it I don't think he ever said anything about his personal history. But I made certain assumptions and came to believe them fact.'

'A common enough practice,' agreed Maltby, resisting an impulse to continue with the whisky. Wouldn't do to be drunk in charge of a child. It would soon be night and the boat; a sleepless night of conversation, he expected, with more drinking. It was good to pace one's alcohol intake on a journey like this.

'Common practise or not, it's a habit I scorn. Stritch's very silence drew you away from the traps of tamed humanity leaving one option, to be wild as he was. I suppose he must have had a mother and father; even Jesus had parents.'

'A virgin mother and vestigial father I believe. Carpenter by trade.'

'Yes,' laughed Est, 'Jesus was found under a sawing horse. I found Stritch under a bush by a river.'

'Did Excalibur appear by any chance?'

'There was no sword, only the small silver knife he used to draw his own blood.'

'In the medieval manner of tortured saints.'

'Let's make up a game to play with Claudia when she wakes,' Est changed the subject.

'Good idea.' Maltby rubbed his eyes after briefly meeting those of the man behind the newspaper. They had forgotten about him as they drank Scotch and talked of blood, suicide and martyrs.

13.2 Loving Godhead

'Why the blazes did you bring the accursed thing here? He has nothing to do with me! What are we supposed to do with it or *him*!' Beast paced up and down as much as he was able in the cluttered bedsitting room of his Order's Paris headquarters. He had returned from the Sahara with Pet some three weeks ago.

'Following orders, my dearest Beast.' Animal crossed her ankles jauntily and filed her nails. She was smug, well groomed and nourished after all that home cooking at Mama Shag's.

'*My* orders! I've never heard such absolute tosh! I was not within one hundred miles of that place!' spat out Beast. He kicked a small Eastern ivory inlaid table out of the way as he fumbled to find his curly pipe. However, he didn't want to smoke the strong mixture of tobacco and hashish. 'Have you got some tobacco, Lillian?' he asked timidly, returning his potent mix to a grubby ruby velvet waistcoat pocket.

Animal raised a neatly plucked eyebrow; that was the first time he'd called her 'Lillian' since she'd first set eyes on his infamous phallus. Was this a sign of lowered defences? Was he stepping off his pedestal? Ipsissimus no longer?

'Don't quiz me Animal, there is no turning back. I couldn't be an ordinary citizen now, I've gone too far into infinity.' He sat loosely in a low chair, low through state of collapse rather than by design. His limbs were arranged elegantly. Stritch in coffin, rested on the floor beside him. Beast rubbed his forehead, contemplating the coffin problem.

'I'll go and find you some tobacco,' offered Lillian, reaching for her coat.

'No, no Animal, stay with me. I don't want to be alone with that box.' Animal giggled. Beast's face was doughy yet majestic with large ears and curved brow.

'Animal.' His hands were smooth and white, legs lightly muscled and feminine. 'You are all I'll ever need. You my beauty, my exotic cabaret all day, every day. My Scarlet Woman, through you my magickal grade is authenticated.' He lit a pipe he had stuffed forgetfully with his strong consciousness altering mix. 'How fascinating you are! Mama Shag has taken good care of you. I will enjoy squeezing your plump buttocks until all the juice runs out.' Beast sucked deeply upon his pipe, his eyelids drooped over brown eyes.

Animal squirmed on the flea infested divan. She was irrevocably contaminated with Beast's needs. She felt his needs as her destiny, that she had been born to ride the Beast bareback, a hand upon a horn for balance.

He smoked the strong mixture of hashish and perique and his composure was restored; he no longer worried about the presence of a dead body. 'Had I been the Archbishop of Canterbury, I could not feel more confident of my relationship with the Loving Godhead.' He decided to himself that it would after all, be easy to bury the box and its unfortunate contents. He wondered that he had ordered it here. He chortled to himself, thinking of parallels with ancient Egyptian magickal rites.

Animal slid a finger between his lips. He sucked upon it; it tasted of salt, cunt salt.

Beast closed his eyes, his stiff neck relaxed on the worn damask. Waves of rich feeling rejuvenated his nervous system. His spine became a writhing snake, uncoiling as Animal's lips enclosed his lingam and tongue flickered over his testicles. He lifted his buttocks so she might pull down his trousers and undergarments to release his partially imprisoned genitalia.

He relaxed entirely, released from responsibility. He let out a huge unembarrassed fart. His body warmed as his heart pumped blood to his extremities, stimulated by action of soft mouth on hard lingam. In fellatio happiness Beast dreamt of his island Abbey, the new home for his Order of Thelema where his teachings would thrive. Their place in the sun.

Animal's tongue ran up and down the underside of Beast's phallus, along the ridge which felt to the tongue, like a scar. The uneven seam extended all the way down Beast's lingam and over his wobbly testicles.

Animal's view was up the phallic slide to the helmet's frill resembling mushroom gills or the scare flare of skin around a dinosaur's neck.

'Is he ever going to come?' thought Animal. Mouth still upon phallus she groped about on the floor, felt under the chair and found her carved wooden dildo. 'I'll thrust it up without moistening it, carpet hair and all. He can't jump up while my mouth is upon him. No man ever fully forgets that a mouth is full of teeth. He'll come instantly.' She tickled his phallus with the tip of her tongue and found his arse hole with her finger.

He eased down in the chair to allow her access. Toying with his tiny anus hairs she noted how distended his anus had become from Pet's dick. 'A right bugger!' she thought with a touch of sexual jealousy she felt guilty about. As Beast's Scarlet Woman jealousy should have been obsolete.

She thrust the dildo into Beast's anus. His contortions and suppressed scream together with hot salty ejaculation, gave her the most delicious mental orgasm, without loss of physical control. She laughed before she swallowed his semen.

She needed more semen. She used the dildo as a piston, withdrawing it completely before reentering Beast's anus. Her mouth teased his testicles.

His body shook; his orgasm subsided and he squirmed away from her mouth.

'I have not finished with you,' she commanded. 'Turn over.'

She felt beneath the divan with a grin bigger than Long John Silver's. She found the double-ended dildo, one end for him and one for her. A dildo that required the skill of a female with superb muscle tone and control.

Animal slipped off her ivory silk camiknickers. She retained her stockings and suspenders and tucked her dress hem into her pastel pink suspender belt to keep it out of the way of the male movements of her narrow hips.

Absentmindedly she brushed a spider off the dildo - the end she nudged into her wet vulva. She removed it and turned it round so both ends were wet and holding on to its carved head with her muscular yoni, she guided the dildo into Beast's arse and did not leave off her crazy gyrations. She was determined to get him off again.

She scolded him, sex talked him, spanked him like a mule. She dug her nails into him, bent forward to bite him; but most of all she rode him. Back arched she rocked to and fro. She beat him with her flat hand and always always she clung on to that dildo and kept it moving inside his arse.

During his fourth plateaux of pleasure Beast heard a tapping coming from the coffin. Animal did not leave off sodomising him. Beast bucked; Animal resisted, riding him rodeo style. He bucked again and again; with each buck his muscles gained power, even as the soft pad of his stomach slapped loosely under him on the chair's threadbare upholstery.

Finally Animal was thrown off to land, buttocks down, with a thump upon the thumping coffin. Saliva dribbled from the corner of her mouth; her hair was straggly with sweat.

Beast's trousers were about his ankles as he cocked his ear to another bang from within the coffin.

'Where is my pipe?' he asked. Animal panted, her eyes wild. She handed him his pipe. Beast put a match to it and then heard another bang.

'Did you hear that?'

Animal quite unexpectedly, exploded into laughter.

'That!' she ejaculated.

'Yes that.' Beast was unperturbed.

'That is our downstairs neighbour banging with a broom on the

161

ceiling to tell us she doesn't like sex noise. The chair legs have been knocking on the floor this past hour.' Her cunt still held on to the dildo; she pulled it out assisted by a push from yoni muscles. She held up the dildo, cream one end brown the other, a slimy trophy. ' Shall I present her with this, as a prize for her efforts?'

Beast chuckled indulgently, puffed on his pipe with his clothing around his ankles. His phallus faded and fell to the left, its skin folded and wrinkled.

They chuckled together. Then came banging from the kitchen. 'That'll be Pet,' Beast declared casually. 'Go and let him out dear Animal; he can drink champagne with us. He hasn't had a drink yet today. I'm training him to do without.' He handed her a key to the packing case in the kitchen.

The kitchen smelt fusty; a tidal scum of rotten food had collected about its edges. Animal bent down in the gloom and unlocked the padlock. At the sound of rattling chains the noises from the box increased and Animal whispered, 'It's alright; only a moment. It's alright; a drink in a minute.'

Pet leapt out and licked her nose with a dry tongue. His tongue lapped at her, searching for wet cunt to appease his thirst. With the wild eyes of humanity forced back to the last reserves of instinct he lapped at her cunt with bestial insistence.

She stroked his wild matted locks, picked out and crushed two large head lice. She scratched behind his ears. The back of his neck was a mass of congealed blood. She let him suck her cunt to dryness but stopped him gently as he searched for her anus.

'It's alright Pet. Come and have champagne. Can you stand?' He had long been crouched in the case and it was hard for him to stand. She helped him to his feet and wrapped a big black woollen cape around his filthy, and in part festering, naked body. He leant heavily upon her as he hobbled into the next room.

Beast stared angrily at them.

Animal shook her head and mouthed, 'Not now.' Beast conceded. Animal gave Pet water to drink. He drank three pints before he was satisfied. She put a pan of water to warm on the stove to wash him.

'I am not going to stay here and watch you molly coddling my trainee. You do know you are undoing weeks of training,' Beast hissed at her. Animal smiled simply and pushed him out of the way.

'You've pulled your trousers up at least,' she said contemptuously. 'Why don't you visit your American sponsor? A telegram came from her.'

'The voluptuous Jane.' Beast smoothed his hair and rotated his huge onyx ring.

'She'll feed you at the best restaurant. You'll enjoy that. Here are your shoes. Remember to tell her she's beautiful and order only the best.'

'Of course, naturally.'

'And don't come back for at least a week.'

Beast took Animal's hands, the nails encrusted with dirt from Pet's behind the ear scum; he kissed her fingers. 'A bientôt,' he said. He looked good, healthy and impressive.

13.3   Paris Families

'I don't want what I treasure of myself saved for occasional ritual use. I don't want my true Will kept in obscurity and labelled "soul," ' Est confided to Maltby. 'I want the best of me available, alert and my genius to be as responsive and finely tuned as my body. As food to my body, I want to be to the world.'

Est turned from the view of Paris where with early autumn, trees turning yellow and red, framed the city. Heart full, she rested on Maltby's shoulder; his camel wool coat was soft and rough simultaneously. She felt new made and expectant since adopting male clothes. Could she bear to be completely female ever again?

Her relationship with Maltby had changed since she'd changed costume. She never would have snuggled up to him when clad in silk underwear, skirts and heels. She'd have felt awkward. How incongruous they must look, a short and a not so short man, embracing. Maltby was more placid than he had been, better groomed too. He always shaved and his eyes didn't dart so from side to side.

Claudia ran up from below the brow of the hill, a deliriously happy girl spinning around with arms stretched out. Then she fell down into chill morning dew. She smashed through the delicacy of cobwebs, a clumsy giant in this fragile morning utopia. She was the encapsulation of fun.

'Fall in love with me.' Est spoke into Maltby's neck, into the piece of shaved skin beside his Adam's apple above his white cravat and cream collar. 'Nail a crucifix in your soul each moment of love you feel for me, until your soul is a mass of tiny crucifixes. My affection will poison our love; your response will destroy my passion. Passion keeps me away from people.' Est shivered despite his manly arm about her curvaceous form.

Claudia rushed into their legs, breaking their temporary union. Est chased after Claudia who called out, 'I'm going to get you. I'm going to get you.'

'No you're not; I can run as fast as the wind,' Est called.

'I can run faster than the speed of light.'

'I can run faster than the speed of time.'

Maltby pottered thoughtfully; he picked at an oak leaf and rolled it between his fingers. It was dry and wouldn't roll into a ball; he flung it away.

The girls came running back to him.

'Is it true? Really true,' panted Claudia, 'that Est's a famous painter and her paintings are selling for thousands and millions of pounds?'

'She's making a fair amount of money.' Maltby placed a protective hand on Claudia's head. 'She'll make more next week I expect.'

He threw back his large head, laughed once or twice as if he didn't quite mean it. He was preoccupied with Est's words.

'Next week and the week after that and the next and the year after, all the way to the millennium and beyond.' Claudia revelled in the intoxication of money after long poverty.

The three strolled hand in hand.

*   *   *

Meanwhile, in a three-room apartment not so far away, Beast returned to his lair where Animal had been nursing Pet. Pet hadn't spoken yet.

'Pet must go back in his crate.' Beast removed new white kid gloves and took off his new mulberry trilby. His devilish forelock was oiled and curled.

With a scurry as quick as a flash, Pet leapt from the divan and darted into the crate.

'Nail down that crate Animal and come attend me.' Beast stalked into the living room, his magickal charisma reaching into every corner, as he measured changes, dangers and resources.

'All is well my Animal.' He pressed her cheek with the palm of his hand and stared into her eyes for one moment. He bit her ear in erotic play to give her pain she would enjoy.

'Don't do that Beast.'

He kissed her lips, held her cheeks tenderly; he was the archetypal seducer and more, in spite of physical degeneration in consequence of excess.

'Later I think I will pay someone.' He drew his lips away from hers. 'There is nothing like a lovely fucking whore, full of lice and chaos.'

'Lice? Are you sure?' Animal poured red wine into two goblets from a bottle she and Pet had opened.

'Full of lies and chaos then, you idiot.' Beast looked about. 'Very cosy,' he remarked, noticing the bottle and goblets.

They swapped signs of enmity over the top of their goblets. Anger, a resource. Hate, an uncharted universe.

'You are so dear Animal.' He drained his goblet. 'So clean yet somehow more unstable than ever.'

Animal raised her eyebrows at this, internally reacting.

'By the way I met your sister today.'

'Yes,' answered Animal coolly, 'she called earlier.' An act of rebellion as Beast had forbidden her sister to visit, on the grounds that she destabilised Animal by artificially awakening her interest in the past, in family.

Beast poured them each another goblet of wine, adding this instance of disobedience to the score chart in his mind.

'I think,' he said, 'we will all meet here. I have asked Jane to call after tea. I believe she is longing to meet you.'

Meeting her sister had made Animal more aware of emotional nuance, jealously included. Raw anger ignited in her ears and fired up her bowels.

'Excuse me, my bowels are moving.'

'In that case, enjoy your bowel movement while I examine the condition of my phallus after a lovely lunch with the luscious Jane. I love to see you jealous Animal, though my Scarlet Woman should not so debase herself.' He poured himself more wine and settled upon the divan with the newspaper and *I Ching*.

13.4   Work

'School? What do you think Claudia?'
'I don't know.' Claudia swung her legs under her dining chair. Upon the dining table before her were coffee, croissants and a pile of bank notes - francs paid for paintings.

'We've got a lot of money now.' Claudia picked up some of the money and eyed it cautiously. 'Are you very famous Est?'

Est laughed. 'Not very famous nor very rich.'

'Yet,' interjected Maltby.

'I'm not going to count my chickens before they're hatched. But you could go to school Claudia, learn French, music, dancing and science.'

'You mean really speak French?'

'Oui.'

'I don't know. Would I be able to get dressed up in white every day and wear a straw hat in summer?'

'If you want to, you can. There won't be paint all over the place at school.'

'I won't be there all the time?'

'Not on Sundays nor the evenings.'

'I'll think about it.'

'Good. Why don't you two visit Miss Jane, an American lady who runs a school for young ladies?'

Est tidied Claudia, instructing her to wash hands and face, brush hair, put her hat on and did she need to wee? Sent her out with Maltby to see Miss Jane's establishment, to stay there for the rest of the day if it seemed pleasant.

With Maltby and Claudia gone Est was left alone in her Paris studio. Maltby had found it for her. It had a high ceiling with a small sleeping area in the rafters. Unbeknownst to them, just round the corner was Beast's pad where the coffin lay and where, that evening, he would assemble with acolytes Animal, Pet and Miss Jane.

The studio was bare, unlived in. It had cream walls, a tiled floor and a small cooking area in an alcove. Four white canvases leant against the west wall; each was ten by six feet, bigger than a king size bed.

Absent mindedly Est removed her tweed jacket and rolled up heavy cream silk sleeves. Her arms were smooth and graceful, her fingers square and powerful. She took the first canvas and propped it against the south wall.

Only a short time ago a canvas of this size had been financially out of the question. It happened in time, did money. The moment before utter destitution was the moment when one became super-charged with transformational energy.

'A generation of evil, a decade of temptation,' Est murmured to herself, scanning the canvas mercilessly. 'I see a head and only a head. It is the head of an immortal heroine from the future. She has not yet had her statue cast in bronze nor placed in a public promenade. She is neither married nor single. She epitomises the cravings of young hearts; she is created from their desire outside hope or possibility.

'Her head is huge and there is no background. She is not born of loneliness or thought. Her origins are in self-loathing and self-mutilation. She succeeds where Faustus failed: she can conjure a demon and take control.

'Material form is irrelevant; my design is about all that cannot be brought to form except through magick. It describes freedom and physical defiance. Freedom is female for I am a woman.'

She worked beside large north facing windows looking out to city rooftops. She picked up drawing materials as she needed them.

'Everlasting nothingness, prosaic, obvious; easy to look at but hard to digest.' She thought.

'Est,' a voice behind her. 'Est.' She sometimes heard her mother's voice calling her; it went away when she thought of something else. 'Est.' This wasn't her mother's voice as it hadn't gone away to order.

She held out her arms and touched either side of the canvas in a brief embrace. A tear collected in the corner of her eye and emotion upset her stomach, for she recognised Stritch's voice.

'The painted face shall bear scars,' she thought aloud, 'all the scars that Stritch bore. It will be the colour and texture of wounds, the emblems of his passion.' She felt cold hands upon her shoulders, lips of ice upon her neck.

'I am your dead demonic lover.' Icy hands rustled her silk shirt, traversed her breast. She shut her eyes, did not want to see, did not want to know how real or unreal these hands were.

'Your contours are part of my personality. Does that mean I love you?' The dismembered voice spoke close to her ear.

'If you could give all barefoot children shoes, would you do that?' a voice in stereo as the ghost hands toyed a moment with her trouser fastening before sliding under the waistband in an explicitly sexual embrace. An ice cold body pressed against her buttocks.

'If you could feed every hungry stomach, would you do that?'

Est opened her eyes; she still stood before the canvas. She could see no hands. The ghostly presence dispersed. She drew a deep breath.

'I will paint in red/purple and red/brown. The picture will be as hot as a ghost is cold.' She visualised Stritch's red wounds, his bruises and blood spattered shroud. 'The reds will suggest non-healing wounds, the very substance of his soul.'

She sat cross legged on the floor and drew wounds in a sketch-book. She propped a mirror in front of her.

She drew herself as a man, then as a woman. She took off her shirt and drew herself in her cami-top, took this off and drew herself topless. She drew her ear. She drew herself as a handsome man and then as an ugly man; as charismatic, business like and then as destitute. She drew her knees, her feet and calves.

The grief of Stritch's death and his semi-realised apparition spread a mist upon Est's consciousness which made her longings easier to transmit to paper and canvas. She did not pause as she usually would, to think. She didn't stop to eat or drink while mixing a range of reds, purples and a little sky blue to pick out veins.

'I can't abide yellow. I will not have any yellow in this picture. I shan't go and spread my legs upon the divan and masturbate either. I shan't think of Stritch's hands. I'll think of the aims I had before I met him; I'll think of The Magician. Why did I formulate a need for The Magician and why did Stritch replace my need for him?'

Est cried guilty, secretive tears for Stritch. Although she knew little about him she remembered their shared passion profoundly.

Her tears cleared as she continued to work on the head. Miniature landscapes sprouted within the space between features, forests of red/purple trees with contorted branches.

'The studio is too small.' She pressed her back against the windows and was still unable to see her painting clearly.

'Nevertheless I shall paint it even though I cannot see it. I shall paint the greater design faithfully and scratch out the details in excruciating pain.'

Thus she continued. Some bank notes blew off the table and fell unnoticed to the floor as light faded to grey. She worked until Maltby and Claudia's return disturbed her. As they opened the door, calling her name, the rest of the banknotes blew to the floor.

'Est!' called Claudia. 'Miss Jane is so tall; you should see her.' She jumped up to kiss her mother. Maltby noticed that Est looked strained and white.

'I have wine; let us drink,' he said.

Est washed her brushes while talking to Claudia. 'Don't,' she said, 'don't touch me yet. My body feels like a bolt of lightning. You know how I get when I'm working.'

'If you're an electric charge, something terrible will happen to you when you touch water.'

'I don't need water for something terrible to happen to me.'

'I'm sorry Claudia.' Est sipped her wine. 'I've been working too long. Tell me how Miss Jane's was. Miss Jane was tall and?'

'Yes she was tall; I don't know what she's like - she wasn't there much. I did some sewing and some singing.'

'Anything else?'

'Some writing. It was easy.'

'Not too easy?'

'No.'

'Do you want to go there again?'

'One of the girls pinched me.'

'I'm sure she didn't mean to.'

'Yes she did. I didn't mind; it was only because I sang better than her. It was quite good. I'd like to go there.'

'Good. Thanks Maltby; you're a marvel.' He had brought in food as well as drink and some paintbrushes and pencils for her.

'Tonight,' he said flamboyantly, 'we shall celebrate this new life, so much better than the old.'

'Much better,' Est and Claudia said simultaneously and laughed at this coincidence.

Chapter 14

14.1   The House of God

Autumnal equinox was more than a month past and darkness
came earlier. Animal sat upon the divan and gazed out of the
window at the brick wall of the neighbouring building. Pet banged
within his box in the kitchen off and on all evening.

Since Beast had left for a bit of whoring Animal had not moved
to anoint Pet's wounds nor to feed or water him. She day dreamed;
wished she were a whore; then Beast would be looking for her.
He'd choose her from the girls on offer at the brothel. She'd be
wearing a sea green silk shift; she'd lift it above her waist and show
him her hips and buttocks. His phallus would rise and he would
do things to her.

Outside in the street a desperate voice roared, 'Animal open the
door. I need you.' She didn't stir. Pebbles ricocheted from the
windowpane. Then tired heavy feet echoed in the stairwell.
Eventually there came a huge thump upon the door as a large body
crashed against it. The apartment shook.

Animal's mouth was dry and sore; she ignored the thump on
the front door. She drained a goblet of red wine and balanced
precariously on the grey kid high heels she still wore. She twisted
her ankle twice before she managed to turn the key to Pet's box.
Inside he lay naked, curled up asleep on straw, a pile of half chewed
cabbage leaves beside him, human excrement in one corner. The
assault upon the front door continued.

Leaving Pet's box open, trancelike Animal turned to the front
door. In the tiny hallway she banged into the free standing coat
rack which rocked and fell. The hall was not wide enough for it to
fall to the floor so it came to rest slanted upon the opposite wall
with Animal beneath it, covered in coats. Thus imprisoned she

could not open the door.

Pet was cold in his opened box. He whimpered, curling and uncurling. The poundings upon the door continued until finally with a splintering crack, the screws came away from wood and the hinges gave way. The door however, moved but a small way, blocked from within by the fallen coat rack.

'If you do not remove the obstacle and let me in, I am going to return with an axe and chop this door into firewood. And I don't care if you're The Beast himself.' A determined Irish brogue.

Pet hopped out of his box and crouched upon his haunches. In excitement his bowels liquefied and he left a trail of diarrhoea behind him as he bunny jumped out of the kitchen.

'Help me - lift this up - it's Mahoney.' Animal tore at the coats, trying to remove them from their hooks.

'I'm going now,' called Mahoney, fifth hound in Beast's pack. 'Going to get an axe.'

'Mahoney it's Animal. The hall stand is blocking the door; it fell over.'

'Lillian is that you?' Mahoney, prepared for the presence of the whole damned sect, was greatly relieved to hear his beloved's familiar voice.

'Yes.'

'Thank god.'

Animal giggled.

'Why do you laugh my love?'

'This is hardly the house of god.'

Pet gesticulated gleefully at the sound of Mahoney's friendly voice, though it hurt him to stretch his legs, used as he was to cramped conditions.

'Animal, can you lift up that coat rack so I can come in? You do not know how I thirst and hunger for you!'

Animal swallowed hard, much affected by his sweet words.

'Pet can you help me?' Pet nodded, grinning ecstatically.

'Stand then,' she instructed. 'Stand and be strong.'

She had heard Beast commanding Pet in this way and seen a sudden, miraculous transformation. She gathered her being in the pit of her stomach and stretched her spine. Above her hung the symbol of Pluto enclosed within an isosceles triangle. She repeated the command, 'Stand and be strong, be deFaustian.'

Pet did not speak nor meet her steady green eyes, but he did rise stiffly, erect and human to join her in a workmanlike manner to push against the hall stand. His lingam with its shaved pubis was massive in contrast to his fleshless hips and thighs. His naked body was smeared and dirty.

He and Animal heaved; the door scraped sorrowfully across the woodblock floor.

'Animal, my very own Lillian, what soulful joy to hold you! In my nightmares I thought I never would see you again.' He kissed her ears, neck, her nose, saving her lips for when his words had all been spent.

'We are not so far from nightmares.' Animal could not summon the icy manner she had adopted in Our Lady's house. Jealousy had weakened her resolve to be totally Beast's Scarlet Woman and no more Lillian. The comfort and reassurance of romance felt easy and pleasant. It was nice to offer her neck to his kisses, to bask in his devotion.

Pet tugged on Mahoney's smart trousers.

'Steady,' Mahoney picked up the stand, 'let's get out of this place; there is the most terrific stench in here. Come on Lillian.'

'No,' she pulled away from him. 'I can't disobey Beast.'

'What do you mean, "I can't disobey Beast"? Of course you can.'

'I can't. You can't either, Hound No.5. Nor do you want to, same as me.'

'What are you talking about? That's the past. Over, door closed.'

Pet whimpered and pointed to the kitchen food cupboard.

'It is not always possible to close doors once they have been opened. As it is not always possible to open closed doors. Look at the state of that door,' Animal said vehemently. She rummaged in the kitchen cupboards to feed Pet. She found a few old biscuits crawling with small beetles; in disgust she tossed them on to the floor. Pet retrieved them and gobbled them greedily, beetles and all.

'At least come to the hotel with me,' Mahoney pleaded.

'Alright,' she conceded. 'I'll bath Pet, we've got to take him with us.'

'What! By a lead attached to that wretched collar around his neck?'

'Do not interfere with matters you do not understand. The pain of your life is as nothing now in contrast to what it will be if you interfere with Beast's work. Not because of Beast's Will but because of fundamental energy. You have no idea of Power; leave well alone. Come.' She had regained her Scarlet Woman composure. 'Let us prepare Pet for the world.' Pet squealed in delight.

Pet licked Animal's ankles; Mahoney groaned.

'Have I spoilt your romantic mood?' queried Animal.

'I don't know,' he remarked while helping her to heat water. 'I don't know much, overwhelmed as I am by the smell of this place.'

'It is rather high, isn't it?' Animal giggled. 'Pet you stink.' Pet nodded, smiling as she sponged his back gently and thoroughly. 'I am going to sponge all the stink off you. I don't think I can sponge all these off though.' She picked a large louse from his hair. 'Help me kill these Hound No.5.'

'This is some infestation.' Mahoney picked through Pet's hair. 'Where do you keep razors Animal?'

'Try under the divan cushions.'

'?'

'Why not? Good a place as any.' They laughed together. Pet scratched his sore hip bones.

'You won't itch soon; you'll feel good.'

Animal dug out some clothes and shoes for Pet from under the divan, the regular store house in this eclectic household. There were some of Mahoney's old clothes that he'd ripped off before vanishing naked into the city night. He'd emerged after surprisingly little incident at Mama Shag's place, *Ridelands*, the other side of the Channel. Such is the strength of attraction when magick and art unite.

The clothes were none too clean but Animal folded up sleeves, belted trousers as best she could and tied a neat tie round Pet's neck.

Pet's legs were weak on first emerging into daylight. He dropped onto all fours squealing in fright then took cover within the folds of Mahoney's cashmere coat. Mahoney coaxed him to his feet while making polite explanations to alarmed passers-by. After all, it was not a crime to be agoraphobic.

On reaching the hotel Pet wanted to go straight to the restaurant. Being a drooling creature with mucous dripping from his nose they persuaded him up to room No.73, where they assured him food could be served and privacy guaranteed. The mention of privacy had a civilising effect upon him, reminding him of former habits.

Animal made the most of the luxury of hot water and prepared Pet a sandalwood scented bath. Pet refused to remove Mahoney's old clothes and ended up getting in the tub fully dressed. He screamed happily as sodden clothes clung to his skin in great wet creases.

Once the plug was pulled, Pet lay in the empty tub and shivered until Mahoney brought him sardines on toast and hot cocoa laced with rum and cream. Pet swallowed awkwardly, for it had been weeks since he'd eaten nourishing food. He'd been living on thin milk and whatever bugs he could find in his crate.

Animal cut the wet clothes off him as Pet would not move to help or hinder her. He lay passively, eyes shut, bony brown hands at rest. He was a pathetic figure indeed, a tiny scared skeletal form in the long porcelain tub. She finally coaxed him out with promises of more hot cocoa and chocolate cake. She wrapped him in a huge towel and stroked his bald scalp, his half healed whip marks matched those on her own body. Exhausted, Pet tottered on to the pink quilted bed. Out of the habit of thought, sleep came easily and he snored, satisfied with his own being.

Animal and Hound No.5 sat beside one another in two comfy armchairs, squeezed in beside the bed. They drank Irish coffee for neither could face the idea of solid food, something to do with the smell of Beast's apartment, No.32, lingering in their clothes.

'It's too late to have a bath,' stated Animal peevishly.

'Past midnight; I doubt we could get hot water.'

'We must go out soon. Beast expects us.' She used the monotone that always angered Hound No. 5.

'What do you mean, "Beast expects us?" ' he burst out, wanting to meet her eyes, confronted instead by her sensual profile - turned up nose, arched brow, ears full of curves and convolutions like seductive baroque ornaments. She used a couple of hairpins to fasten back loose strands of hair.

'Are you going to file your nails now, maybe pick your teeth and pluck your eyebrows?' Hound No.5's angry outbursts never lasted long.

'Pet must come to No. 32. Jane will be there.'

'What has Jane being there got to do with Pet coming?'

'Have you met Jane?'

'Jane?' Mahoney was confused. 'I don't know, I'm not sure.'

'I haven't met her,' stated Animal simply. 'Beast is using her to bring me back to him. He's been concerned he's losing me because of you. I am jealous of her.' She didn't sound jealous at all.

They sat companionably quiet, waiting for the time to wake Pet, when they could go back to No.32.

As Pet snored, Hound No.5 and Animal watched him curling and stretching, disconcerted by the lack of his box's definite boundary. His legs thrashed a while then he let out a hearty fart, its mouldy fruit and veg stench filled the room.

'Yuk!' Hound No.5 and Animal exclaimed simultaneously; then

linked little fingers, said 'jinx' for luck and wished.

Pet's fart released a pool of watery diarrhoea which quickly soaked into the pristine quilt.

Animal sighed, 'We can't leave it.' However, it was Hound No.5 who got up from his chair to begin the messy process of cleaning up.

'I'll stuff him with white rolls and bread tomorrow,' Animal said sleepily, curling up for a snooze in the damson damask chair.

Pet did not waken throughout the cleaning process, not even as Hound No.5 cleaned his anus. Open and bare it was, pathetically exposed as there was no flesh or muscle upon the buttocks.

Hound No.5 took the quilt and the blanket out from under Pet's fragile form, rolled them together and left them in the bath. He eased Pet back in to the middle of the bed, fascinated by Pet's arse. The thinness of the buttocks added to its attractiveness as did the testicles which hung hairless beneath.

Right by the arse hole was a small tattooed sigil. It was hard to make out the exact design. Hound No.5 switched on the bedside light to examine the mark; it was a sigil he had not seen before. He drew out his long tongue and licked it, feeling the ridges of its design. It tasted soapy and shit bitter. He drew his tongue across the anus, poking it slightly into the arse hole as he passed by and on across to a second sigil. This was slightly larger, its design simple. He recognised it as the sign he'd seen above the door of the kitchen in No.32, a Pluto symbol enclosed within an isosceles triangle.

His tongue moved back to Pet's anus and licked around it, poked his tongue into it. Very excited he pulled Pet's buttocks apart - he wanted to shag Pet. He was sore from excitement, he just had to shag Pet.

Pet did not stir as Hound No.5 tore off his trousers and mounted Pet. 'Got to shag Pet, got to shag Pet.' He said over and over, his lingam sore from desire even while he was shagging him.

Pet did not wake but Lillian the Animal did. Propped up on an elbow she gazed on at Hound's antics with feline complacency.

Catlike, she slunk to the window to close the curtains. She unwound a long knotted leather whip from around her waist where it served as a belt.

She teased the leather with her fingers. Her pelvis rotated erotically as she drew the whip serpentine along the floor. She whispered sex words to the whip and wrapped some of its length around her hand.

She could tell by Hound's grunt and rhythm that he was nearing climax. He looked piggy edible, his pink buttocks clean and freckled, cute, so smackable. She bit him gently on each buttock. She timed her bite carefully so his thrust would not knock her in the face. She stood back and lifted the whip and brought it down to inflict hurt upon his fat, decadent bottom.

The blow was accurate; a painful red welt rose across flesh. Hound No.5 leapt off Pet.

'What did you do that for? I was about to come.' He shook with anger.

'Coming up Pet's arse, were you?' she smirked. 'Wouldn't that be rape?'

'But - we're consenting adults,' babbled Hound No.5.

'Consenting adults?' questioned Animal, pointing with a long fingernail at the oblivious Pet. She raised the whip decisively with her right arm. 'Lie down.'

He obeyed meekly. The penny dropped; consenting adults had nothing to do with it. ' Us,' he said to himself. He was becoming one of 'them'. Inside, his stomach felt different, more alive, challenged and powerful. He was serene as Animal whipped him.

'Imagine,' he said to himself, 'imagine pain feeling so good; yet it does.'

'Remove your shirt,' commanded Animal.

It felt good to obey her, to know that he was Hound No.5, that he wanted to be Hound No.5. With this new self came the confidence to change his life for the better. 'Us!' he cried each time the whip fell upon his back, buttocks and legs.

Animal delivered the thrashing that marked the first stage of transition from man to creature, while another initiate, Pet, underwent the reverse transition, from creature to man.

14.2 Sex Action

Pet awakened around midday the following day, Friday 2nd December, after one more incident of somnolent diarrhoea. Sleeping, shitting and being shagged by Hound No.5 had done him good, whatever that meant. His face was tranquil and he had recovered the power of speech. His joints were stiff and he was ravenous. He recognised Animal too, which he had not done the day before.

'Why the deuce am I bald?' He sat bolt upright upon the bed, now stripped of bedding, all of it having been piled up in the bath soiled with shit. The smell of it wafted in through from the ensuite bathroom.

'And what is that god awful stench? Shove over Animal.' He nudged her and hurt his shoulder socket. 'Ouch! What have I been up to?' He examined his body, the body of a gargoyle, emaciated with huge erect penis. 'My arse is so sore Animal.' She lay on her side facing away from him still wearing silk stockings. Her face was stained with purple lipstick. Pet rubbed at the lipstick marks which merely smeared, as the paint was thick and greasy.

'Wake up Animal, wake up,' Pet repeated. She threw her arm out and turned over onto her back, banging against him.

'Sleep then,' he yelled in her ear. Animal's dry lips moved together once or twice: 'Drugs. My throat!'

Pet rubbed his neck. 'Christ! I am so thin! How did I get this thin? And this big!' His penis grew more, pulling out of his foreskin, the head big and purple. 'Christ, what a steamer!'

A knock on the door. 'Breakfast as ordered.'

'Damn it,' he said to himself. 'Un moment, s'il vous plait.' He hopped out of the bed, his legs at first collapsing under him. 'Christ what am I like?' He picked himself up and struggled into a black silk robe embroidered with a fiery Chinese dragon. He opened the hotel room door a crack and took the tray from the red and black uniform of room service, who raised an eyebrow.

'Must have spotted the body on the floor,' thought Pet.

'Is Monsieur Mahoney okay?' inquired room service, trying to look round Pet into the room.

'Just fell out of bed. I didn't want to disturb him.' Pet took the tray and hurriedly shut the door.

Pet tucked into coffee and croissant. As he finished the pot of coffee his bowels began to move, he only just made it to the lavatory. A rat ran out of the bath and under a skirting board. 'Christ.' Pet's bowels emptied, spattering the sides of the pan with half digested food. 'In one end, out the other.' His guts heaved at the appalling smell coming from the soiled bed clothes piled up in the bath. 'One thing at a time,' Pet told himself in vain attempt to delay vomiting until he got his head over the lavatory pan. He didn't make it though, and puked up coffee and croissant all over the baby blue chenille bath mat.

'Bugger it. Cock sucking tarts being buggered by school boys in shorts with scuffed knees!'

He dumped the bath mat into the bath and flushed his shit away; it rose up out of the water before it vanished.

A part of him felt inclined to lick the lavatory seat clean, another part retched at the idea. There were awful aches in unlikely parts of his body.

He saw the rat again; its nose peeped out from the hole it had disappeared into earlier. Pet backed off and shut the bathroom door behind him, hard. He opened the sash window to let in some fresh air and city sounds. The dirty city smell was welcome after the highly personal smell of his own guts.

His erection came on again, the one that had drooped when that chap with the brekka had rapped on the door. 'Definitely the same one,' he remarked as his lingam pointed up to his face like a deadly missile, purple and determined.

'Christ, where did you come from? What am I going to do with you?'

Hound No.5 and Animal lay as before, on the floor and on the bed respectively.

'Animal the delectable cunt, my darling wife,' Pet's heart raced. 'Provocative, tempting cunt, sex wet and muscular, I want to get in you.' He hopped up onto the bed and crouched in front of her, as Hound No.5 had crouched in front of him. 'Animal, cunt, Animal.' He shook her. 'Sod you, or not to sod you, shall I pierce your lips with this? Or shall I part the furry lips of your vulva to encounter the smooth wet passageway that never lies?'

No response. His greedy fingers pulled up her skirt, pressed her thigh flesh, pressed her pussy. One greedy thumb pressed into her vulva and a finger into her anus.

'Animal you well used woman you, let me use you.' He squeezed her breast through her silk dress and chemise.

'Stritch!' she murmured as Pet squatted astride her with the tip of his purple penis dabbing against her clitoris. He opened her labia majora slightly, using his penis head to find her love bud.

'Nice, Animal. Very nice.' He stayed poised thus, waiting for her to wake. He could feel the signs of her arousal and her lips moved, but still she slept. 'He's going to go in you.' Pet's penis was unstoppable. 'Can you feel that? Now he's slipping in. Can you feel that? I can Animal. I could stop if you didn't like it; I could but I'm not stopping, I'm slipping into you until I'm all the way in.' Arousal rippled through him and his lingam grew in Animal's yoni as her muscles grasped hold of him. 'Pull me right into your pretty pussy.'

Hound No.5 sat bolt upright. ' What's that?' Very awake. 'Get off her, you disgusting fiend! You vile lecherous dog!'

Pet laughed softly and groaned, easing his penis very slowly, pulling against Animal's internal hold on him; then he let go, to be taken more fully within her. His testicles bobbed gently against her. He laughed, as Hound's sandy mane stood messily up on end, his face smeared with Animal's purple lipstick.

'Get off her, you simply cannot do that to my...'

Pet laughed softly.

Hound No.5 remembered his act of buggery upon Pet and the steam of his protest evaporated. There were no rules, no etiquette of sexual behaviour amongst them. It was not a matter of consenting adults, more a matter of thorough exploration of psychosexual impulses, to find the instincts that lay beneath sexual convention and discover a new world beyond instinct, a magickal world.

Hound No.5 crouched close to watch lingam inside yoni. He licked the rim where they joined, licked the shaft of Pet's penis, tongued Animal's clitoris, both directly and through its miniature foreskin.

Voices outside the door passed unnoticed by the engrossed trio - a whispered exchange before a handle turned quietly and a syrupy, brown sugar voice resonant with rich inner resource addressed them.

'Well, now, what have we here? What lovely scene meets my eye this fair Friday?'

14.3   Voyeurs

Beast rubbed his fleshy ringed fingers in subtle gesture. 'Please continue. I would not want to interrupt you.' A soft knock upon the door. 'Jane, you may come in.' She slipped in and stood right up against Beast as if a powerful magnet stuck her body to his. She wore a long sheath dress of thick brown satin. This longer garment heralded a new fashion direction. Her hips were full and round; the dress did not flatter her.

'I insist you continue.' Beast surveyed the room hawkishly. 'Dear little Pet remount our beloved Animal; I believe our Hound No.5 wishes to gloat more upon your coital action.' Pet had withered in the presence of His Holy Bestial One. He'd crawled off behind an armchair with cupped hands incompletely covering his rod of passion.

Jane slid her hands up and down Beast's maroon suited back.

'You are kind and attentive,' he purred. Though his pleasure in Jane was more related to the size and accessibility of her purse than the action of her hands, for Beast had a dream to fulfil. A dream of a place where his people could live together under The Law of Love and the authority of The Beast. A place in the sun where children could be begotten and reared to become the first generation of Love, his Magickal Children.

His dream had become clear of late. Red robed children clambered across rocks, gathered flowers, chanted poems celebrating Pan - goat god of passion who knew no emotion other than ecstasy and so annihilated the instability of changing emotions. Consistent and continuous ecstasy was thus the gateway to Beast's Thelemic Order.

Beast, in his occult journey, had discovered new aspects of the human psyche. He had translated the unknowable into words and numbers; he knew how to describe what was not.

Jane slithered against Beast's back. She pressed her mount of

Venus into his buttocks.

'Jane,' Beast instructed, 'take that whip lying upon the floor and use it upon the parts of Pet you can reach until he comes out from his dirty hiding place and mounts the lusty Animal. He will always come out for a good whipping, won't you, my little Pet?'

'Very well,' agreed Jane with an American twang to her voice, reluctant to pluck herself from Beast's person.

'Were you hoping I would to impregnate you here and now, Miss Jane?' asked Beast loudly, embarrassing her. Miss Jane was not yet used to the Thelemites' uninhibited ways, although they made her vagina throb. She picked up the whip and laid two accurate lashes across the soles of Pet's feet. This brought him out eagerly from behind the chair, lingam ready to go.

Hound No.5 and Animal had not moved nor spoken. He crouched, she was spread eagled. Both salivated.

'Bugger her you big boy, bugger her,' shouted Beast to Pet, who whimpered pathetically.

'Don't you want your prick up her arse?' Beast's eyes flashed with the beginnings of unearthly energy. Pet shook his head.

'You stand upon your hind legs and shake your head as I recommend anal sex with Animal? Would you rather crouch on all fours and have this Hound No.5 thrust his pulsing rod of Pan into your quaking shit filled arse?'

Pet nodded and grinned showing dirty chipped teeth.

Beast threw his head back and howled, a guttural howl of instinct and passion, a sound to waken dead energy, medieval memories. To conjure the essence of fear.

'We are together,' Beast boomed musically. His words vibrated through every person and every object in the ordinary hotel room. 'Not to do what we want to do but to do what is right: to harmonise our bodies with divine energy: to synchronise our lives with the future universe. This will not be done half heartedly, nor will it be done without pain. What comes hardest to us is what reaps most reward.

'Bugger that Lady Pet, bugger her good. Do what is repulsive, do what is challenging. Do what stirs vile feelings and thus shall feeling be annihilated.

'Bugger her Pet. We shall not do what we like, we shall do what we must do. We shall do what we Will.' His spine shivered, satisfied as Pet mounted Animal's arse and Miss Jane laid two deep cuts upon Pet's skinny back.

'Today,' Beast continued, 'is our Miss Jane's naming day. I wish her to experience everything we have experienced. I wish her to know everything we know. She shall be one of us, shall share in our ecstasy.'

'Yes please Beast,' smirked Miss Jane.

'He shall strip you; we shall whip you. Using a hot branding iron to scorch your flesh where it is ripe and tender, we shall lay our mark indelibly upon each buttock.

'Then we shall dance naked. We shall cavort and rub our genitals upon each other's bodies. We shall be drunk with Love and wine and we shall all have sexual intercourse with you this night. We will show no mercy; we will stop at nothing. Are you ready to join us Miss Jane? Are you ready to have your body smeared with the juices of our priestess's sacred yoni, to give your body to Loving free expression? To be absolutely free from morals and guilt? Are you ready for your naming day Miss Jane?'

Miss Jane pressed her thighs together as he spoke, while Pet rhythmically buggered Animal and the bed creaked. Hound No.5, on all fours had moved to Beast's side and licked his hand, while Beast played with Hound No.5's thick hair.

As Beast's speech had progressed Miss Jane's hands had unconsciously travelled to her vulva which she rubbed, at first slightly and discreetly, then had got her fingers right in there.

'I am ready,' she coughed out in high excitement.

'Prepare the pipes,' Beast ordered Hound No.5. 'First we will smoke. If anyone knocks on the door - hear me Animal? If anyone knocks on the door you are to answer it naked and offer them sex. Understand? Offer them sex, hear me?' An answering grunt came from the bed.

'I will be interested to see how you fare my dear.' He patted Miss Jane's hand paternally. 'Let's get your clothes off now, shall we my dear?' She nodded, choked. 'Let us hope it is just before your time of ovulation, when you will be most hot to trot.'

Beast took a long silver knife and thoughtfully ran a fat finger along the razor sharp blade; he drew blood. He held his bleeding fingers up and shook drops of blood around the room, mumbling exotic words.

With one strong gesture he swept the clutter off the coffee table and ceremoniously laid down his knife on the thus prepared surface. He took a long candle and drew it under his nose, smelling its honey-tinged beeswax. He chanted a mantra as he lit it.

'By the time I turn around Miss Jane must be naked. You, Hound No.5, remove her clothes and bring them to me when I ring this sweet little bell.' Beast resumed his exotic chant. From his pocket he took a long pipe, a tobacco pouch, a small packet of greyish brown powder and a small leather pouch. In deep concentration he laid all the objects carefully on the table.

'I need the naked Jane,' he said, his back to the others on the bed. Pet ejaculated noisily up Animal. Beast paid them no attention. He cooked up the powder in a spoon over the candle until it dissolved. He was careful not to let it evaporate. He took a 20ml hypodermic syringe from the small leather pouch and filled it with the heroin mixture.

He hummed; the hotel room was fast filling with his atmosphere, squashing out its day to day ordinariness.

*   *   *

While the group in the hotel located veins to have a hit, Est knocked on No.32, Beast's apartment, round the corner from her own studio flat and not so very far from the hotel. She had received a message via Maltby that a collector had bought one of her paintings, would probably buy more and would like to meet her. He'd been told she was male. This collector was Drummond, Beast 666 and Est was calling on him, by appointment at 4 o'clock p.m..

'Hello,' she called to no reply. 'Hello?' Hello is pretty similar in French and English, it's a matter of intonation. She pricked up her ears and heard a rat-like scurrying sound from within the apartment.

On the off chance she tried the door, which to her surprise, opened. She screwed her nose up at the smell of urine and vomit.

'Why,' she said to herself, 'a decomposing corpse could not smell worse.' She thought momentarily of Stritch, then put the thought determinedly from her mind as she considered whether to enter, foul smell and all. It was dark inside.

'Hello?' she called again. 'Is anybody there? This feels like a game of ouija,' she thought. She stepped back and looked down the stairwell but there was no sign of Drummond. Curious, she decided to step into the apartment. If anyone turned up she would simply tell them that she'd found the door open and stepped in to wait. 'That's true anyway.' She peered through to the gloomy front room, stepped over wine bottles left lying haphazardly upon the floor and picked her way over to the window to open the curtains and let in what daylight remained.

'My god.' There was no sign of domestication, as if a pack of wild animals had just sloped off to hunt. Bed clothes, dirty glasses, dog ends were strewn about. Books lay open revealing red wine stained pages. Underwear and high heeled shoes were flung around.

There was an old mattress in the middle of the room and most startling of all - a coffin before her, from where she assumed, came the foul smell. She thought again of Stritch, his hollow purple eyes and his erect lingam entering her swollen vulva.

Her knees were weak as she pushed away images of Stritch and knelt beside the coffin. She tested the lid; thirteen nails were nailed half way down and easy to lift out. She lifted off the heavy lid. Cradled within blood stained cream satin was Stritch. She was aghast. His eyes and nostrils squirmed with maggots. There were deep holes in the palms of his hands, where he had been nailed to the crucifix and his neck looked broken, for his head lay at an unhappy angle.

His flesh was warm with writhing maggot life. She gagged and tried to replace the coffin lid but could not, for her stomach contracted. She puked all over the floor. With shaking hands she eventually lifted the coffin lid and with bangs she felt could be heard at the other end of the world, knocked the nails back in place using a heavy book which lay beside her, Beast's well worn copy of the *I Ching*, by the by.

Est didn't notice what book it was. Her heart raced as she panicked. She could hear a thousand feet returning to the apartment, a thousand voices asking her what she was doing here.

She wondered why Stritch was here; she knew no causal link between him and the art collector Drummond. She only knew through Maltby, that Drummond was English, rich, pretentious, bad tempered but easily humoured.

She was paralysed, for although she wanted to leave this place - not be here for whoever might return - she felt compelled to stay with Stritch's body. She couldn't leave him here to be eaten by maggots without proper burial.

An emptiness spread within her. Her body ceased to be important as anxiety dissolved. She felt at one with this entity who had shagged, talked and cried. Stritch who had kissed her with Destiny's kiss of togetherness. She felt close to his true spirit and luxuriated in his company. 'Even dead, he's fun to be with,' she thought.

14.4 Angels of Elation

It was deep in the night when the carousing sex party returned to No.32 for wine and recline after being chucked out of the hotel for making excessive noise and trashing the room.

Est heard the elated clamour of Beast and his horde, but did not react. She knelt before the sealed coffin; passion within her was a molten orange flow.

She thought of Stritch. 'Are you The Magician of whom I dreamt night after night, searched for along concrete corridors, each door at first glance identical to the last, until I came to a door and put out my hand and the door opened? I had seen thousands of doors but was only attracted to this one.

'Vitality soaked through my skin as I passed through the doorway into a green world where I merged with Stritch. Are you The Magician for whom I search? Are you he whose power and influence I paint?'

Before a reply came, the marauding horde poured in. The wobbly coat stand fell on them as they entered, just as it had fallen on Animal the previous day. Coats and cloaks heaped on top of them and Beast's horde laughed in great whoops of chaotic self expression.

'Who is that?' Est called.

Beast, Animal, Hound No.5, Pet and Miss Jane were piled up in a panting heap.

'Ouch, get off me you wanton savage.'

'Wanton savage, yes, and more! I will, with my savage teeth, bite bits from you.'

'Is this your flesh?'

'It's mine. Enough!' called Beast.

A quietening. 'Good. What do I see before me? A mournful figure kneeling before the coffin of our dear departed sacrifice. Be quiet as you follow me for I feel our time of completion is near.

She is come for special reason.'

Throwing his robe from him Beast stepped proudly naked into the main room of the apartment. A few birds chirped outside the window; one accidentally threw itself against the windowpane.

'You have come,' he said with monumental satisfaction.

Est looked up at him, his soft hanging stomach his slippery retreating penis, his enlarged fleshy breasts with well developed nipples, strong sinewy muscles on slim limbs of girlish delicacy and elegance. He held out ten fat fingers, sparkling with green and purple jewels. He showed her the submissive underside of his hands. Like a jellyfish, the soft underparts were where he carried his sting.

Est took his hands and with vacuous momentum, all that she was flowed into Beast. He drew the knowledge she had acquired during her astral journeys, into his eyes, as he would drink wine.

'Yes, indeed,' he nodded.

Now another wave came from Est, not a giving out but a taking in, a backwash to his swash, a natural equivalent to her gift of revelation. He was dumbfounded as she became dark and demanding within his consciousness and sucked on *his* power.

She knew the answer to the question she had asked Stritch. For here he was, The Magician who had sucked upon her dreams night after night. The Magician who had watched aeons flow through the entity Est. Watched her gather power for this encounter outside the order of time. Now they met in the here and now in a Paris room, on each side of the coffin bearing the human sacrifice necessary before this meeting could happen.

Tears welled in Est's eyes; she wept for her beloved Stritch as he had been, warm alive and loving her, leaving her.

'You killed him,' her voice was dry and level.

'Let us see.' Beast swelled and his skin flushed. Est felt a strong impulse to reach over and embrace him, impale herself athletically upon his lingam.

'Animal, a cloak.' Animal had crawled out from the pile of

collapsed textiles where she'd been having a bit of a heart to heart and a kissing session with Pet, much to Hound's annoyance. Hound No.5 had felt very left out and even more annoyed at Miss Jane's stroking condolences. She was no substitute for Animal; he hated her broken veins, her crows feet, massive clitoris and scabby knees. 'Some women,' he thought to himself, 'need expensive clothes so much.'

Helpful Animal passed Beast a heavy maroon velvet wrap lined gorgeously in black silk; it rustled against his skin as he secured it round his shoulders. She found a sumptuous cloak for each of them.

'You say I killed him?' queried Beast.

Est raised the hard white line of her chin in assent, as birds chirruped with the rising sun.

'Animal, remove the nails from this coffin.' Animal found a knife. Beast and Est were absorbed in one another.

'We could be one person,' she said lightly with a hint of criticism.

'We are that one person we both wish to become,' Beast replied ecstatically. 'We have both become that one person.'

Animal removed the last nail from the coffin and she and Beast lifted the lid together.

What they now saw in the coffin was not what Est had witnessed earlier. For a start there was no foul smell. The group of cloaked acolytes gathered around the coffin. At first the box seemed empty. Then a tiny figure formed from smoke that seeped like sweat vaporising from the bodies of each of the gathered company. The tiny figure was translucent at first like a seahorse, but it grew with the group's breath. As it grew it writhed in the cocoon of vapour that enclosed it. Gradually it became opaque and three dimensional. It grew and grew and with the first ray of true yellow sunlight on the morning of Saturday the 3rd December, Stritch stepped out from his coffin with a lovely smile on his face.

'My Est.' He took her shocked body in his arms, more humanly warm than he'd ever been before. Est was not sure what to think.

'So I killed him, did I?' challenged Beast, his eyes flashing with fun.

'Can you feel his living hand, warm in yours?' Beast asked Est.

'Yes, I can. I can feel his fingers interwoven with mine and the change of texture from skin to nail.'

'Can you feel the pulse of his heart in his wrist?'

'Yes, I can.'

'Then he must be alive.'

'It is a resurrection,' declared Est. 'He who was dead, lives. He whom I thought was lost has come to me. Just as I have found you Drummond.'

'Beast, my dear, please.' He patted her hand, the one that was joined to Stritch's. 'The difference between life and death is not what you suppose. You will of course be coming to our Place of Prophecy?' He paused for a reaction. 'Our Dreamhouse of Destiny?' Another pause. 'Our Abbey?

'Let us have breakfast. I am ravenous,' he continued, assuming her assent. 'Animal, Pet, make yourselves decent; you need to go shopping. Werewolves need to eat too. It is good to tear one's clothes off and make free with one's body. It is good to shag and be shagged. It is good to lay aside thought. It is good too, to fill one's belly.

'Est, I believe you are called; join us for breakfast. Then you and your daughter must prepare yourselves for an important journey as honoured companions of Beast.

'When we arrive I shall impregnate my women and we shall have Magickal Children. Come to me, my love.'

Beast wrapped his arms around Est who utterly relaxed in his embrace. His body was rank with sexsmell of rampant wild human, evoking distant memories of life before civilisation.

'Where is he?' Est asked.

'Who do you mean, my dearest love?'

'Stritch.' A name that made her throat palpitate.

'Dead. Gone from here. We have taken the coffin away.'

'Not two minutes ago he was beside me.' Beast ran his hands down her back and held her buttocks. Pressed his pelvis against her, smelt her hair.

'You have been against my body long enough for a burial to proceed and a breakfast prepared. Can you smell the coffee steaming in the kitchen?' Beast's voice was empathetic, more soothing than a lover's; she had to trust him. He knew her so completely that to refuse to trust him would be to refuse to trust herself.

She had searched for him and she had found him and she must rejoice. If the future revealed him evil, so be it. She would go with him to his Place of Prophecy, surely a more interesting place to grow for Claudia than Miss Jane's decorous establishment?

'Where is he?' she asked quietly.

'I can't answer that. I can say that his body has been decently buried. I cannot say how much of him, if any, rests.'

'I see.' Est smelt coffee. Beast released her.

'Coffee, breakfast,' he announced. 'You have surpassed yourselves. Miss Jane how adorable you look naked and quivering in the morning light! Come sit on my knee and dip a croissant into your coffee. The compote is very good, Est. Have you met Animal, Pet and Hound No.5? I know you are already acquainted with Miss Jane. We shall do so much together. Don't you think Animal?'

'Perhaps,' Animal answered nonchalantly. 'You are usually right Beast.'

'We shall have fun,' Animal assured Est. 'We shall create the Magickal Child.'

14.5 Beast's Ambition

'Our Abbey shall stand on top of a hill covered with olive groves and bush oregano. In the valley below, nectarines and tomatoes will grow in profusion. The scent of these succulent fruits and woody herbs shall be carried upon a benign breeze through the archways of our Abbey.

'Animal shall play whimsical tunes upon the flute to mark dawn, noon and dark. There will be no preset patterns to our sleeping and our waking, for we shall work as True Will instructs. We shall not surrender ourselves to unconsciousness; we shall remain alert at every hour. For every hour is sacred and deserves our full attention.

'And I shall calculate the exact hour when our children, The Children of Thelema, shall be conceived.

'We shall all participate in the conception; the seed will be plentiful, Venus brilliant and the full moon sinister.

'Love shall reign and our spirits will be free, our liberation created from the sticky stuff of dreams in which I am wholly immersed. I can hardly tear the cobweb filaments of surreal images away from my eyes sufficiently to see the day's task of animal survival ahead.

'Miss Jane! You must take care of us all, be our mother, the fountain of abundant nourishment. Come, sit upon my lap, feel my lingam rise beneath your monumental buttocks as I massage your blooming bosom. Feel how I tear cloth from your skin and lay your breast bare. Feel how stiff my rod grows beneath your buttocks. My lingam writhes with independent life, straining to reach your fertile tunnel.

'Pet, Hound, both come! We must honour Miss Jane's natural abundance with the tribute of our masculinity. Come penetrate her moist furrow with your tongues and your fingers, while I tease her nipples.' Beast had not forgotten that Miss Jane needed special, initiatory, attention.

'Lay bare her skin! Excite her beyond levels of ordinary endurance!'

Animal was curled up asleep in a corner with her thumb in her mouth. Pet and Hound No.5 snorted, doggily eager to part Miss Jane's heavy thighs and prise pleasure from parts of her that had previously been anxious and cautious. The lady who had volunteered to give freely of her rich purse to fund The Abbey of Love would also freely give her sex juice and orgasms.

Beast worked cocaine into her nipples. He numbed them with pure excitement as he squeezed them hard. Pet worked cocaine into her clitoris and her anus, his fingers rubbed and probed while Hound No.5 was busy with his tongue, licking up cocaine as he went.

'Excuse me, I must be off now.' Est felt awkward, but nobody took any notice of her. She had to go and have breakfast with Claudia and Maltby before she took Claudia to school. Not that she'd be taught by Miss Jane today by the look of her decadent posture. 'Three serving her! Who'd believe it?' Est leapt down the stairs three and four at a time, the three flights to street level.

Chapter 15

15.1 Genius At Work

'What do you think? Bright blue sky plus heat?' enthused Est, walking Claudia to school while Maltby went about his business of selling Est's paintings and handling her escalating success.

'I don't know about heat,' Claudia responded.

'Not hot all the time, mainly warm.'

'I like warm. I don't know about blue. I like grey sky and clouds.'

'You and your grey sky! Don't you love it when the whole world explodes with colour, when trees you think you know well take on a new beauty?'

'I do know what you mean Est. I get that feeling when I look at your paintings.'

'Really?' Claudia and Est strolled by the schoolyard wall of Miss Jane's establishment.

'Yes I do. Your paintings are very vibrant.'

' "Very vibrant". You are a one Claudia.' Est was impressed by her daughter's ability to express herself. 'Goodbye ma cherie. Be good. Learn a lot. Have a lovely day.'

'Don't worry, I will,' called back Claudia after her goodbye kiss.

Est waited until Claudia disappeared into school. Other girls arrived, mainly accompanied by governesses who looked disapprovingly upon Est, dressed up as a stout and tousled gentleman.

Returning home, Maltby had left a note on the table. It read: 'Gone to sell 1,000 paintings from the brush of a genius. Love Mxxx.' Est smiled thoughtfully, deciding whether to paint in the gloomy kitchen or the light room. Whatever; paint she would, energetically and prolifically.

It would not be long now until the sect of Love removed bodily to their Abbey. She didn't suppose Maltby would come with them. Not a great user of his penis, Maltby, she thought, as she mixed a brilliant orange down to a luminous rust. She took off her shirt, her vest and breast squashing brassiere. She propped a mirror next to the canvas. She wanted to paint her breasts today, first interpreted as a male chest, in warm rust and then as female in green turquoise and brown maroon. A third painting would merge the two impressions.

An electrical shiver shifted her awareness of self from her creative core within her pelvis to her nerve endings. The tip of her tongue grated on a rough tooth.

'I still do not know if Stritch is alive or dead.' She stared blankly out of the window of the dark kitchen where she had decided to paint; it was even tinier than her English kitchen. They had moved fast; she hardly knew where she was. Since arriving she'd only had time to paint, not time to know Paris. As success became the dominant factor in her life, she seemed to slip across the surface of life.

'I can't cry when I don't know if he's dead or alive.' She sketched, painted and sketched. She wanted to make love with Stritch. She remembered their precious lovemaking in minute detail; he was the best. 'Best' turned to 'Beast' in her mind as images turned to language.

Symbols kaleidoscoped in her mind, appearing first as chaotic letters in infinite space, then arranging themselves into words. 'I have found him. He is my Magician. He is mine. I will never let him go. He is my Beast and through him I can find what I have always looked for within myself. I will surpass my genius.' She would use this fresh enlightenment to further articulate the source of her inspiration. Her talent had a fierce momentum; it was variously rare, tough, sensitive, ambivalent, offering a visionary version of time, stirring lusty, yet refined passion.

Est roused herself from her topless bout of painting just in time to pick Claudia up from school. She was still dazed from the discovery of new strands to her sense of origin and destiny. Also, she was not looking forward to telling Maltby that she and Claudia were leaving Paris to live in an experimental community.

'Did you have a nice day?' Est took Claudia's schoolbag for her.

'Lovely.'

'So good that you'd feel bad about leaving?'

'Are you serious about going to this warm place?' Claudia squinted at the low winter sun.

'Yes, I think I am.'

Back at the studio Est made Claudia a warm milky drink. Claudia surveyed Est's work.

'If going to this new Abbey place makes you paint pictures as beautiful as these, we shall have to go shan't we?'

'They're not finished. They're still wet.'

'Did you do all these today?' Claudia turned from one to another.

'I haven't finished them yet.'

Claudia threw herself into Est's arms. 'Est they are beautiful! Will it be as wonderful as all that?'

'I think so my darling. I really do think so.'

'Then I'll go with you, even if it means leaving Maltby behind.'

15.2   A Walk On The Wild Darkside

'What will I do without you?'
'Don't be so corny. You can come and visit us.'
Est and Maltby drank red wine in two shabby easy chairs in Est's studio. Claudia slept in the sleeping space in the eaves above.

'When it comes to it, you won't want to see me,' Maltby sulked.

'We shall need money! I shall need to sell my paintings!'

'Is that all you want me for?' he sulked. 'So you'll still be painting?'

'Mais naturellement.'

'You say so now.'

'Come on Maltby. I've painted through thick and thin, hell and high water; I'm hardly likely to give up now.'

'Probably not.'

'Well then?'

'You'll be in another world; there will be more distance between us than that made up of fields, mountains and the Mediterranean Sea.'

'Beautiful countryside will separate us; beautiful feelings will bring us together.' Est was dizzy and did not sound sensible. In spite of her intention to reassure, her extravagant star-struck mood unsettled him. He twirled his empty wine glass around by its stem.

'You know I am devoted to you and to Claudia. Wherever you are, you will always come first in my life.'

'Dearest Maltby.' Est accepted his offer of a refill but did not give him her full attention. Her rosy glow was not in consequence of drinking Bordeaux with Maltby; it was because Beast had raised the veil between herself and the world and herself and her soul, and the world had rushed into her soul.

'I will come and see you once a month to collect paintings, provide comment, pass on criticism, money, news.' Maltby sat forward, his head in his hands. Est noticed that he was thinner, paler. His belt was done up two notches tighter than the worn tan marks upon the leather indicated was its usual position.

'Are you *very* worried about us?'

His sweater was worn thin at the elbows. Usually he looked so smart in suit and sparkling white shirt.

'Most likely more than I can say.' His voice was husky with wine. He still didn't look at her. 'You are taking a considerable risk.'

Est laughed lightly to conceal that she was psychologically

wrong-footed by Maltby's concern. 'What is life without risk? How can one ever discover light without moving occasionally into darkness?'

'But darkness is darkness and light is light. Of what possible use can what is found within darkness be, except to those who are committed to a life within darkness?' Maltby's voice varied between enthusiasm and resignation. He was not, in any case, at home talking on philosophical matters, only forced to do so to express what was on his mind, as Est's life was crossing over from the practical sphere into the experimental, where, empiricist that he was, he couldn't follow her.

Est laughed awkwardly. 'Although a walk into the wild darkside may seem like the rash action of one purchasing a one way ticket to purgatory, I know that with Beast's guidance and influence I can gather from the darkness what I can find nowhere else. If I wish to shine light into the dark corners of my perception, I can only do so only when I have dared to tread where I cannot see,' she explained.

'Only the blind truly see! Now you're being corny.'

'There is a difference between what is lame and corny (the words and acts of an apologist) and what taps into the eternal pool of knowledge.'

'So you will step out from darkness, a livid lake of thick engine oil that is Beast's Abbey, as the Lady of the Lake, carrying the sword of deliverance, aware of the whereabouts of the Holy Graal. And why Beast? Why do you call him that? That isn't a name; it's a debased condition.'

'Dearest Maltby, you are angry. Shall I run my fingers though your hair to comfort? Put my arm about your shoulders. Shall I kiss you gently on the lips?'

It was quiet in the studio.

'You don't sound like yourself. You sound like you're being taken over by an evil entity,' Maltby dared to say.

Est's laugh was angry now.

'You don't sound like yourself. Are you the same person? Is Beast's influence finally piercing through your thick skin? Evil entity! Huh!'

'I'm sorry Est. I don't want to argue. Your going away has challenged my feelings for you. I didn't know I felt so protective. This friendship touches my heart more than I knew.'

'You could come with us?' She knew he wouldn't.

'Orgies, resurrection and prolonged eye contact are not, I am afraid, my cup of tea.' His eyes briefly met hers.

Dawn was breaking; they had both cheered up.

'Let's finish the bottle,' he suggested. 'Nice wine, don't you think?'

End of Book I

~